✦An Angel's Noel✦

Knight to King 4: The Fischer-Kasparov Match

The Nation's Hope

To the Close of the Age

✦An Angel's Noel✦

Kenneth T. Zemsky

Cover art adapted from *Bob Cratchit and Tiny Tim at Church,* by Jessie Wilcox Smith.

Cataloguing-in-Publication Data

Zemsky, Kenneth T., author.

An Angel's Noel/Kenneth T. Zemsky

Pages cm

ISBN: 9781977504494

1. Christianity. 2. Angels. 3. Christmas inspiration—Fiction. Title: An Angel's Noel.

Designed by Grace Anthony

Summary: Christmas is approaching and God is sad because of all the evil in the world. To cheer Him, the archangels send Tommy, the newest angel, back to earth to find five instances of people performing random acts of peace and goodwill. Complicating matters: the heavenly emissary's supernatural powers are not fully developed yet, everyone he comes in contact with is inordinately surly, and he is burdened with a secret from his prior life. Can the angel fulfill his mission in time for Christmas?

Printed in the United States of America.

To Grace, Richard, Marisa, Christine and Caroline

See that you do not despise one of these little ones. For I tell you that their angels in heaven always see the face of my Father in heaven.
MATTHEW 18:10

He spake well who said that graves
are the footprints of angels.
HENRY WADSWORTH LONGFELLOW

Angels patch the holes in our hearts.
TERRI GUILLEMETS

Those who believe in Jesus never see
each other for the last time
TOMMY, THE LITTLE ANGEL

✦One✦

When Tommy was very, very little, he beheld the face of God. Now, of course, he saw God regularly. The funny thing was God looked nothing like how Tommy remembered Him.

Tommy thought of this as he dutifully entered the throne room. Not that there was any throne. God was all-powerful, but He was not ostentatious. The throne room was just what the heavenly host called it. As Tommy walked in, God smiled and said, "Ah! How's My little angel?"

Tommy liked it when God said this. Partly because it was surely a good thing to be on the right side of the Almighty. But also because that was what Tommy's mother used to call him. Even now it made him feel all warm and bubbly inside to hear the use of her pet name for him. Tommy figured God probably realized that.

The little angel rose from genuflecting and his mind again pictured the God of his long-ago imagining. It was from a picture book Tommy's mother had given him as a gift one Christmas entitled "Children's Bible Stories." In it, God was depicted as an old man. Not old and frail, but powerful with long white hair and a beard. He had piercing blue eyes, flowing robes, muscles and a face that was at once wise, kindly, strong and serene.

In reality, God was not like that. Oh, he was wise, powerful and kind, but His countenance was vastly different. Tommy struggled to put it into words. God looked as complex as the universe He had created. Beyond that Tommy could venture no better description. Human words did not exist to allow for such a thing. The sight of God was one of the things reserved only to citizens of the hereafter.

Tommy also remembered how afraid he had been the first time he had been summoned to the throne room. Back then Michael the Archangel had calmed the little angel's fears, and once Tommy was in the Lord's presence he was filled with such a feeling of peace that he wondered how he could ever have been so naive as to be fearful of God's goodness. That first time was not so long ago; Tommy had arrived here relatively recently. Since then he had been to the throne room numerous times. God always liked to check up on the new angels, to be sure they were happy and adjusting well. That was why, when God today asked how he was, Tommy knew it was a deep and sincere question. He told God in reply that he was happy and doing quite well, thank you.

"Well, soon you will be going on your first mission," the Lord commented. "We have not chosen what it will be yet, but it will happen soon."

"Will it be to Earth?" Tommy asked.

"Yes, in all likelihood," God answered. "To Earth." When He said this, he made a faint expression, almost like a wince, and lowered his gaze, His smile sad.

Tommy asked what was wrong.

God looked up. "Oh, it is just that I wonder sometimes at what has become of what I created. We are getting close to Christmas. At this time of year, if ever, they should remember to be full of cheer and good will to men. But look at them."

God shared the vision of the world with the little angel. In one spot soldiers were fighting and killing one another. In another place as well. "And look at this one," God said, still in that sad tone, directing Tommy's gaze. "This is Bethlehem." Not only were partisans killing each other in Jesus' birthplace, God explained, "They say they are doing it in the name of their God."

Tommy was puzzled. "Since I have been here I have learned a lot more about Your teachings. And I have never heard You say anything about killing one's fellow man."

God nodded. "Exactly."

"Don't feel bad," Tommy said, trying to reassure Him. "Wars happen. They go away."

"It is not just a few wars," God gently corrected the angel. "Look here…and here…and here."

The scenes unfolding before Tommy were myriad. Thieves stole goods in the cities and hurt their victims. Husbands and wives acted hatefully toward each other. Former friends refused to talk to each other because of something trivial one had said, even though now they could not even recall what it had been… or who had said it. Others were consumed with worshipping at the altar of greed. Some people fighting for this wealth were in the business world, and they used practices that gratuitously hurt their fellow members. It was an "anything goes" mentality. Nor were the innocents, the children of the globe, spared. In large regions of the world, children were starving. These unfortunate kids had distended bellies, stick-like limbs and vacant looks in their eyes. Richer people knew about this, but did nothing to alleviate the suffering. Even in well-to-do countries, children were neglected, left to sit in front of televisions or computers, unloved, the cold metal boxes before them unable to provide any emotional warmth. In still other places, little children were horribly abused in ways Tommy had never fathomed. He was shocked to see that some of the perpetrators were ones who abused their roles as teachers, coaches and even ministers to prey on the helpless.

God closed up the vision. Tommy could feel the heaviness of God's heart as He slowly enunciated, "There…is…so…much…hate."

"But, Lord," Tommy said, "people will soon be getting ready for Christmas. They will certainly be better behaved this time of the year."

God sighed. "They are going through the motions, but this people has lost the meaning. Look." Then God revealed another sight.

It was a magnificent shopping mall like the one near where Tommy had lived. Several people were close to fisticuffs over the scant remaining parking spaces. Inside, one mother angrily shoved another so she could get the last mechanical wonder, this year's "must-have" gift. Elsewhere people were taking the Lord's name in vain as they stood in long lines at the registers. Pickpockets stole at least one widow's mite. A father slapped his crying child. Tommy could hear the slap from here. It was that hard. A sign in one of the stores boldly proclaimed, "X-mas sale!"

"X-mas!" God harrumphed. "Do you think any of them appreciates the meaning of it all?" He asked rhetorically. "I sent Jesus to show them a more excellent way, and still they choose to follow the path of the Evil One."

Tommy had a question, but he sensed now was not the time. He let God go on.

"Jingle, jangle, jungle! They are too consumed with themselves to help each other."

Tommy felt bad. He so wanted to say something to make God happy. Impulsively, he hugged the Lord. God smiled at him and again said, "My little angel." Then Tommy pointed out all the good things that had been done in God's name. All the beautiful churches and statues. The art and the music. "Why," he said, "there is nothing more sacred than a Christmas carol."

God shook His head. "This people has grown entirely too cynical. They take all the things you have just mentioned for granted. Listen to a typical radio station this time of year. Do you think you will hear a carol dedicated to peace and love?

Or is it more likely to be about reindeer, grinches or roasting chestnuts over a fire? Everywhere they refuse to see the deeper meaning behind it all. Their hearts have become hardened and they have turned from Me."

"Surely not all, Lord."

"No, not all," God agreed. "But the hatred seems to be in the ascendancy. Why, I suspect any five people you approach at random will embrace the dark path rather than the ways of love." He paused a moment before adding, "The best we had to offer...the Mother Theresas, Padre Pios, Norman Vincent Peales...they are all up here now. Where will the next come from?" He snorted. "Fifteen billion years since the creation and this...," here God made a dismissive wave of His hand toward Earth, "is what we have come up with. It is enough to make Me question the gift of free will."

Tommy scratched his head. He so wanted to be helpful. He thought of the Bible stories he had heard from his mother. She always said when you were confronted with life's difficult choices, the answer was in the Good Book. "I know," he brightened. "You could send a great flood. Like you did in Noah's time. Wipe all the evil away, Lord, and start over."

God shook His head. "No. It would be wrong to punish the few good-hearted people. Besides, I promised never to send a deluge again."

"Fire? Brimstone? Locusts?" the little angel tried again... despite the fact he did not have a clue what brimstone was, though it sounded pretty horrific.

"No, my little angel," God smiled. "You are missing the point. We are not in the business of destruction. Our mission is to embrace creation. Do you understand, little one?"

Tommy looked up, something he usually did when he was thinking deeply. "You mean, doing like Jesus did, loving our neighbor? Even when they are hurting us?"

God hugged His angel. "That is exactly what I mean."

Tommy frowned. "You could force them to be good. Why, You can do anything!"

"I could, but love is not to be forced. Love is patient. It is kind. It must be freely chosen. It cannot be a matter of compulsion."

Tommy thought. He repeated. "Love is patient and kind. Like You!" he brightened. "That's 'cause You are love—right?"

The Almighty allowed a slight indulgent nod.

"What if You visited Earth?" Tommy next asked.

"No. I tried that. When I sent my only Son."

"Who they crucified," Tommy realized sadly.

His answer was met with another Almighty nod.

"Well," said Tommy, "if You can't punish them, won't force them and won't send a direct messenger, what else is there to be done?"

"Hope," God replied. "We hope that what goodness is there will be fruitful and multiply."

They were interrupted by a gentle sound. It was Saint Peter. He had come to discuss arrangements for a large new batch of heavenly dwellers. It seemed an earthquake, magnitude 8.2, had wreaked considerable destruction in the eastern hemisphere and many souls would be knocking at the pearly gates in short order. Tommy realized his interview was at an end as other matters had to be attended to.

"Well," Tommy stammered. "I hope You feel better."

"Oh, little angel, thank you," the Lord said. "You have made Me feel better already."

Tommy felt a little better himself, but he knew deep down God was still troubled. And that still bothered the little angel.

Tommy was next due to meet with the other angels. He still had a lot to learn about being an angel. As he headed to his meeting, he enjoyed looking at his relatively new surroundings. The place was really getting spruced up. Apparently heaven was prepared for Christmas just as homes and businesses on Earth were, except in heaven there were no trees, colored lights, tinsel or lawn ornaments. The heavenly ornamentation was sublime in an otherworldly sort of way. And up here Christmas was more like a birthday party for God, which in a sense is what Christmas should have been about all along.

Yet to call it a birthday party denigrated the festivities. At least in human terms. For example, there was no birthday cake. There were no candles that could mark the Lord's longevity. At its core, Christmas was a celebration during which all the choirs of heaven paid special homage to the King of Kings. Tommy hoped the festivities would cheer the Lord, but somehow he did not think so. God's melancholy was too profound to be assuaged by a mere party. Oh, if there were only some way he could help! He was at a loss, however. Tommy resolved to bring it up with Michael and the other angels in case they had not noticed God's sadness. Perhaps they would know what to do.

While Tommy headed to the gathering place, he passed all sorts of people. Except for the unfortunate few who were consigned to the nether world, everyone who had ever lived ended up here. That was part of what made it such a fascinating place. You were constantly running into souls who had so much to share. The first day Tommy actually met Abraham Lincoln and had been mesmerized. He had once read a book about Lincoln, and Tommy's mother had told him a lot about the president. Lincoln was very kind to Tommy and spent much time talking to him. He had a bunch of funny stories he liked to share. The president also enjoyed hearing about Tommy's young life as much as Tommy was enthralled to learn of life in Civil War America.

Tommy realized that with all the billions of people who lived here, with fresh recruits arriving daily, there was no shortage of lives to be vicariously experienced and thrilled by.

Not everyone up here was famous like President Lincoln. Tommy enjoyed spending time just as much with other children who had died in different times. Just the other day he had spent the afternoon with a young girl who had lived in medieval times. Her stories about knights, farming, castles and the such were like a storybook to Tommy, as were his stories to her.

Then there were tons of relatives Tommy did not know he even had. His grandma was here. He knew her a little. But there were so many great-grandparents and cousins who had gone before. Indeed, Tommy had an incredibly long line of family that amazed the little angel.

Grandma was especially happy to see Tommy. He remembered her as a kindly old lady, but his memory had dimmed. Grandma had died when Tommy was four years old. Now, however, it all came back to him. What a wonderful woman Grandma truly was!

One of the best things about being with Grandma was she was able to share all sorts of stories with Tommy about his mother.

Grandma also had stories about Tommy's father, but they were not as robust as those concerning Mom. That was because Grandma's knowledge of Dad started from when he first dated Tommy's mother. That left a huge gap of Dad's childhood, adolescence and young adult years. Tommy figured he would eventually locate a distant relative from his father's side of the family, and they would provide intimate and welcome details of Dad's early years. For now, however, Tommy was thrilled to sit at Grandma's side and be regaled by stories of Mom as a young girl. Funny, it had never dawned on Tommy that Mom once would have been as young as he was. He should have known that, but he never had. It was as if in his mind Mom and Dad had sprung Zeus-like from the Creator's forehead as fully formed adults.

The stories about Mom were warm and funny and left Tommy immersed in his mother's love despite the time and distance between them.

One of Grandma's stories was about a Christmas party she and Granddad had hosted when Mom was a very little girl. Granddad worked in the accounting department of Georgetown University in Washington, and Grandma worked in the registrar's office. This was years ago. Back then they lived in Northern Virginia just outside Washington, DC, where the university is located. Anyway, they were hosting a holiday party for friends and colleagues from the school. Mom and her sister, Tommy's Aunt Debra, were about three years old. They were fraternal twins.

Mom was fascinated by the colorful-looking drinks the guests were enjoying and mentioned as much to one of the partygoers. When Grandma and Granddad were occupied the guest, who happened to be the chair of the theology department oddly enough, allowed Mom to have a sip of his drink. It was very sweet and Mom liked it a lot. So she started roaming from couple to couple, cadging sips. "A lot of sips," Grandma related, as the evening wore on. Some of the drinks were quite bitter and Mom made a funny face, which the guests took to be unbearably cute. Other drinks were sweet, like the first one, and Mom tended to take a second sip of these.

After a while the room started spinning and she announced she had to go to bed and the bathroom, not necessarily in that order. As she walked across the living room carpet, she started to sink into the floor. As she slipped slow motion to the floor, Mom said, "I can't stands up no more."

The guests loved it, though Grandma and Granddad were less than pleased. Though now after all these years, Grandma laughed as richly over the tale as Tommy did in the imagining. "Your mom had one queen of a headache," Grandma explained. "At least it accomplished something good. She never developed a taste for alcohol." Tommy had to admit that was true, for he knew Mommy never touched the spirituous beverages. This episode was typical of the stories and the images of his mother that enraptured Tommy.

Often after one of these sessions, Tommy would look down from Heaven to check up on Mom and Dad. By way of explanation it is improper in a strict sense to say that heaven is "up" and the angels and saints "look down" on the world. Where heaven is, there is no "up." Old perceptions, however, like habits, die hard, and Tommy, like so many of his new kin, still thought of it as looking down when he gazed upon the world he had left behind.

Tommy felt so much love for his parents he checked up on Mom and Dad several times a day. As wonderful as existence in heaven was, it was when Tommy did "look down" that he experienced the only thing that even remotely approached sadness. That was because whenever Tommy chanced to glance at Mom and Dad, they were inconsolably melancholy. Mom's tears were especially strong. Dad was just as sad, but for his wife's sake he tried to keep a stiff upper lip. The reason for their sorrow was because of how Tommy had come to be in heaven.

Even now, as he watched them, it seemed as though Mom was crying uncontrollably. Dad's eyes were red as he gently stroked Mom's heaving shoulders. But he could not console her.

Nor was Mom eating well. She had lost weight in just these few days. It was noticeable to Tommy, who was also alarmed at how drawn his mother appeared. Months before Tommy left, Mom and Dad had shared the news that Mommy was expecting a baby. Soon Tommy would have a new baby brother or sister. Mommy was not noticeably pregnant then, but now he could see that her belly was getting larger. Tommy did not know a lot about childbirth. There were lots of things he was learning in heaven, but child care had yet to be revealed in the Book of Wisdom. However, the little angel did intuitively grasp that for the baby's sake Mom needed to keep up her strength via nourishment, rest and peace of mind. It would be awful if Mommy was so distraught that something bad happened to the unborn child.

It tugged at Tommy's heart. How could it not? He desperately wished there was something he could do. He had forgotten to bring this up with God. God being so sad had pushed other ideas out of Tommy's mind. The little angel made up his mind to raise this with Archangel Michael. Surely there was something they could do to help Mom. And Dad.

You see, Tommy knew the reason for their sorrow. At the heart of the matter, it was all about Tommy.

When Tommy had been born, the doctors discovered he had a rare blood disease. There was no known treatment for it. Just after Tommy's sixth birthday, the disorder shifted from remission to an active stage. Tommy did not feel much. Just a small and constant tiring as his body slowly shut down. Even at his young age, Tommy realized what was happening. He was only a little afraid. Not a lot, because of all Mom and his teachers had taught him about heaven. So Tommy figured he would be okay. There was some trepidation over the unknown, but it was manageable. Besides, when the time between the realms came so close, Tommy was in such an exhausted state, he did not really care about the matter.

How it happened did come as a surprise to Tommy. He always figured there would be some cataclysmic event or foreshadowing, probably an initial burst of pain and then a void. What happened instead was as peaceful as could be. He just fell asleep. A moment later he opened his eyes, totally refreshed, more so than it seemed than he had ever been. There was an incredibly bright light. It was whiter than anything he had ever seen or imagined and beautiful in a way he could not describe. Tommy wanted to follow the heavenly light and he did. The trip was far but did not seem long. He never looked back. At the end, Tommy was greeted by a kindly looking bearded man. Kind of broad shouldered. The man had deep furrows beneath his eyes.

"Who are you?" Tommy asked the nice man.

The older gentleman smiled and tugged at his robes. "I am Saint Peter. Here to check you in."

"Oh!" Tommy exclaimed. "You're Jesus' friend."

Peter chuckled. He consulted his notes.

"It says here you are six years old, Tommy. Right?"

Tommy straightened up proudly. "Six and three-quarters."

Simon Peter smiled. "Six and three-quarters," he emphasized the three-quarters. "Why, you are really a big young man." The apostle then explained that everyone up here was either an angel or a saint.

"Gosh. Everyone? Not just you and Saint Francis…and Saint Thomas?" Tommy was referring to Thomas Aquinas, his namesake. Mom had always had a fondness for the intellectual Doctor of the Church.

Peter laughed. "That is a common misconception. People assume that only the famous ones who have been canonized are sainted. The truth is all who enter these pearly gates have attained sainthood status. That is why when a loved one dies, the survivors are never alone. They can always pray to their new saint."

"Are the prayers always heard?" Tommy inquired.

"Usually. You will be learning about that in short order."

"Wow," Tommy exhaled. "So I am a saint now?"

"Well, not exactly," Saint Peter said.

Before the apostle could continue with his explanation, Tommy interrupted. "But you said everyone up here is a saint."

"No," Peter gently corrected, putting his hand on Tommy's shoulder. "I said everyone up here is either an angel or a saint."

Tommy looked behind him. One way. Then the other. Since he did not see what he was looking for he told the saint, "I don't have wings so I'm not an angel."

Peter gave out quite a belly laugh. "Wings! Oh, I forget sometimes how quaint human notions are!" Then his eyes crinkled as he looked at Tommy. "Being an angel is not about wings. Those will come later. Angels are chosen by God for reasons known only to Him. One of His rules that we do know is that anyone arriving here who has not reached the age of reason automatically enters the angelic corps."

Tommy asked if that was like the Peace Corps.

Peter said it was exceedingly peaceful, but not exactly like any gathering on Earth. He then asked if Tommy knew what the age of reason referred to.

Tommy involuntarily looked upward and stuck his tongue out as he pondered. Then he remembered that in Sunday school his teacher had said when you became seven years old you reached the age of reason. She added that although some of the children in the class would soon hit age seven, she doubted if they would experience sound reason even when they reached seventy. Tommy did not understand what she was getting at but when he told Mom she laughed. This was just before his final illness kicked in. Tommy told Peter that he understood about the age of reason.

"Very good," Saint Peter observed. He added, "Since you are not yet seven, you will become an angel right away."

"Will I get wings?"

Again Peter gave his belly laugh. "Again with the wings. In due time. Why is everyone fixated with wings?"

"It would be so neat to fly," Tommy observed.

"I guess it would," Peter said, chuckling again. "But you do realize that up here we all can fly. There is no gravity in heaven."

Gravity was an alien concept to Tommy's six and three-quarter-year-old mind, but flying in heaven was not. To demonstrate, Simon Peter floated above the new little angel.

Tommy just wished it—and then he was flying alongside Saint Peter as well. "Cool," he whisper-exclaimed.

"Yes," Peter agreed as he drifted back. "Cool." The word sounded strange in his tongue. That was not how people spoke in Peter's day. The apostle explained to Tommy that flying would take on an extra dimension once he did earn his wings.

From there Peter summoned someone. It turned out to be another angel who was also quite young—maybe not even six and three-quarters, Tommy thought. The angel looked familiar in some way to Tommy, though he knew he had never been formally (or informally) introduced. "How could he be so familiar?" Tommy wondered.

The tiny angel introduced himself. He was very friendly. "I am Jesse. I've been up here since biblical times. For the last six years, however, my job has been to shadow and protect you. You see, Tommy, I'm your guardian angel."

"Is that why I recognize you?"

Jesse nodded.

"Wow! My very own guardian angel." Tommy remembered the prayer he had been taught:

"Angel of God, my guardian dear

Through whom God's love commits me here.

Ever this day be at my side,

To light and guard, to rule and guide."

Peter and Jesse joined Tommy in his concluding "Amen."

Jesse explained that everyone has a guardian angel. "That is why people are never alone, no matter how bleak things may seem. Unless they choose to be. Too many living persons close off their hearts to us," Jesse said. "But not you," he smiled happily at his former charge. "That's why you're perfect for the angelic host."

Then Tommy realized something. He looked back to Saint Peter, who was listening in on the exchange. Motioning to Jesse's back, Tommy told Saint Peter, "Hey, he has wings!"

Peter told Jesse, "You work with him!" and he was off, but in a spirit of good nature.

Jesse said it had taken a while to earn the wings, but Tommy should rest assured. The wings would come in due course.

"They really look neat," Tommy said. "Can I touch them?"

Jesse allowed that he could and giggled quietly when Tommy stroked the feathery things. "It tickles a little," he confided. Then he led Tommy off for orientation. Jesse showed Tommy the entire heavenly realm and helped Tommy get his bearings. When Jesse asked Tommy who he wanted to meet, Tommy's first two choices were Grandma and Abraham Lincoln. Jesse said he would arrange it, and as we have seen, he did so promptly. Then it was time to meet with the leaders of the angel corps. They were in a separate room that had a lot of fluffy clouds, a lot like Tommy had imagined.

There were clusters of angels in the room. Three stood out in particular. The Archangel Michael, the leader of the pack, was the tallest and the strongest looking. He also had the mightiest wing span. He was flanked by two other archangels Tommy had heard of, Gabriel and Raphael.

"Gosh!" Tommy exclaimed, approaching Gabriel. "You're the one who visited Mary and announced to her that she would bear God's Son."

Gabriel smiled. "Guilty as charged."

"Guilty?" Raphael repeated, puzzled.

Then Raphael turned to Tommy and said, "He has done quite a few other amazing things in his time." Gabriel looked down a little sheepishly.

The archangelic triumvirate explained to Tommy what his life would be like now and what his training would consist of. Jesse would continue in the guardian role a while longer until Tommy was a full-fledged member of the heavenly host.

Since that first day it had been a joyous whirlwind. Tommy felt he was learning so much. He barely had time to think about what his life had been like back on Earth. Except on those occasions when he heard Mom's and Dad's prayers and looked down on them. As noted before, these were the only times he experienced anything close to melancholy. Solely for his parents' sake.

Which today he had intended to voice with God, until he saw God had problems of His own.

Right now Tommy was due for an all-wings meeting, and he figured this was the time to discuss both the God problem and the parent problem with the other angels.

The little angel arrived just as Michael called the meeting to order. Jesse had saved a seat for Tommy. Gabriel and Raphael sat to the right and left of Michael, respectively, the trio in front to run the meeting.

"I have a serious matter to discuss," Michael said, "but as is our tradition, are there any agenda items any of you wishes to bring up first?"

The angels looked from one to the other. No one raised a hand or a wing. Tommy hesitantly raised his. There was a murmur because traditionally the new guy did not speak until his seventh meeting.

"Uh, I have two items," Tommy said.

Michael nodded expectantly.

"The first is, I just came from a meeting with Our Father."

"Yes," Raphael said. "Your orientation session."

Tommy nodded. "It seemed to me that God was sad."

There was another series of murmurings.

"God? Sad? It cannot be," one angel said.

"He is a young angel. He must be mistaken," said another.

"I had not noticed anything wrong with the Lord," said yet another.

A few others were exchanging knowing glances. They did not have to give voice to their ruminations, because Michael took the lead, as he often did.

"Very good, Tommy," he proclaimed. "That is precisely the matter I wanted to raise. A number of us have perceived melancholy in the Almighty. Because of the sorry state, the irreligious state, of Earth."

"But it's Christmas time down there also," an angel in the back asserted.

Raphael spoke up. "You mean X-mas. Because they have crossed out the meaning and the spirit of the season."

Another angel Tommy did not yet know said, "Advent just started. Perhaps they need more time. It is a season of reflection."

Michael held forth. "That means nothing down there. To show how sacrilegious they have become, the merchants have taken over things. Halloween and Christmas get mixed up. By that I mean before the Halloween stuff is down, the X-mas barrage starts. It's all a fight for the consumer dollar."

Raphael pointed out that even Halloween had become perverted. "It is supposed to be All Hallow's, the night before the day honoring all saints. Do you see them paying homage to any saints?" he thundered. "No. It's all candy, witches, devils and assorted weird costumes."

There was a collective tsk-tsking.

Gabriel made a funny face and said, "I am partial to the ghost costumes. It's really funny putting a sheet over your head and yelling 'Boo!'"

Raphael shook his head. "It's a wonder with you as the messenger that Mary agreed to become the Mother of God."

Gabriel was about to shout "Boo!" at Raphael until he was silenced by a sharp rap of Michael's flaming sword.

"The problem goes deeper than that," Michael said. He pointed to the general secularization of the holy day. "Jesus has been practically banished from the celebration. In many places crèche scenes are not even permitted. It reflects what is in…or not in…their hearts."

Everyone finally admitted it was a sorry state of affairs. No wonder God was distressed.

Someone asked if the Lord had been in this deep a funk before.

"Twice in my experience," Michael said. "Once when they tortured and murdered Jesus. That was two thousand years ago. The other notable time was in the sixteenth century, when His Earthly emissaries, the popes, were perpetrating massive abuses."

"Thank God for Luther," Gabriel sighed.

"We did," Raphael reminded him.

"Oh, yeah," Gabriel said.

"How about in the beginning?" someone asked. "When you guys had the great battle against Lucifer?"

Michael, Gabriel and Raphael all appeared to shake off a chill. Though successful, thank God, they obviously still bore the scars of that apocalyptic battle.

"This is worse," Michael answered at last. "You see, God knew what He had in Lucifer and his minions. But this…this is a gradual and emphatic rejection of all the love the Lord has shown them!"

Suddenly there were thousands of separate discussions going on at once. In each there was a common thread: it was a downright tragedy—God did not deserve this. God was too good to be dealt even a scintilla of misery.

There was another thunder-like rap of the archangel's sword. The flame flared outward. "Angels! Angels! Listen up!" Michael called over the din. This had the immediate and desired effect of silencing the heavenly host. "We need to work together to come up with a solution. What do we do to make God happy?

Near the front an angel said, "Michael, it is that time of the year for our annual celebration in His honor."

"Boo-yah!" Gabriel cried out joyously. "Party time!"

Through clenched teeth Michael admonished, "Cut out the shenanigans or I will deal with you privately later."

Gabriel looked down. "Sorry, Michael," he whispered. "I did not intend harm."

"I know," the leader said as he gently squeezed his lieutenant's shoulder.

Then Michael spoke to the masses. "A celebration is fine, but it is not the answer. We are talking about the Creator of all things, not a lounge lizard."

"True," Raphael said. "Remember seven centuries ago when we had the deceased entertainers all sing 'Happy Birthday' to Him? That did not go over well."

"Yes," Michael grimaced. "Who came up with *that* idea?" He looked pointedly at Gabriel, who suddenly was endlessly engrossed in studying a particle of the cloud formation at his feet.

Another angel had an idea. "I know we can't send Jesus back, not until the Second Coming at least, but what if we choose a special heavenly emissary? How about Saint Nicholas?"

"Are you kidding?" Raphael said. "Have you seen Nick lately? He is also devastated over the commercialization of Christmas. Santa Claus this and Santa Claus that. The whole chimney and reindeer thing and presents…gimmee…gimmee…gimmee!"

Gabriel added, "It's a good thing Nick is up here. If he were still alive, this'd kill him."

Michael glared at him, but Gabriel stood his ground. "Well, it's true!"

Other ideas popped up. A modern version of the plagues to winnow out the evildoers, for one.

That did not generate a lot of support. One angelic commentator asked them to remember Hurricane Katrina. "The rich all escaped and left the poor to deal with the devastation."

"How about a different kind of sign?" another angel proposed.

"What kind of sign? Comets? Meteors? They'd just start fighting over whether it was heaven sent or the result of natural scientific forces," another complained. She added, "For this stiff-necked people, it would have to be a sign that could hit them over the head like a two-by-four."

"Even if we did that," another opined, "they would drape an arch over the sign and charge admission."

Someone threw out the idea of another apparition. Surely the Blessed Mother would be willing.

One of the wags acidly remarked, "Yeah, like the whole human race has embraced Fatima and Lourdes. The impact will be too minor since they lack faith."

"Well, *we* believe," the first angel insisted.

"You're preaching to the choir, which is not our target demographic," the other responded, and the consensus was clearly with him.

Michael proposed they take a break and pray on it and reassemble in short order. Perhaps inspiration would strike.

As they broke, Jesse asked Tommy, "What did you think of it?"

"Pretty exciting. A little different from what I expected," Tommy confessed. He added, "I think Gabriel is kind of funny."

Jesse nodded. "Gabriel is a hero to most of us. He wasn't always so carefree, though."

"What happened?"

The guardian angel got a serious look. "In the great battle at the beginning of time…the one between the archangels and Lucifer…"

Tommy nodded rapidly. This was thrilling!

"Well, at one point, Satan got the drop on Michael and Raphael. He was about to hurl a deadly thunderbolt at them. From out of nowhere, it seemed, Gabriel jumped in and took the shot meant for them."

"Wow!" Tommy said in wonder. Then he realized. "But you said it was a deadly shot?"

Jesse made a hand motion for Tommy to wait while he finished the story.

"It was a fatal blow. Killed Gabriel. It is said that when Michael and Raphael saw what had happened to their friend, they fought with a righteous fury never seen before or since."

While Jesse paused to take a breath Tommy asked, "But if Gabriel was killed...?"

"He was," Jesse explained. "Immediately after the battle, Michael and Raphael came back for their brother angel's body. They each cried an ocean over him."

Tommy said he had heard that saying before.

"Not a saying," Jesse replied. "Where do you think the Atlantic and Pacific oceans came from? That is when they were formed. From angels' tears."

Tommy's eyes were still wide as Jesse continued. "God has always been tender in the face of good works. When He saw Michael and Raphael's love, and what Gabriel had sacrificed for his friends, God brought Gabriel back to life. Ever since, Gabriel has been a little more, um, carefree. Michael sometimes rides him when he acts up, but don't be fooled. Those three are as tight as could be." Jesse held his three middle fingers together when he said this.

Then the two got back to the matter at hand: what to do about God and the un-Christmas spirit down on Earth. They kicked around a couple of ideas, but nothing hit home. It was the same problem the many groupings of angels were having all over the hereafter.

"It's too bad we can't come up with some incredibly tremendous good work," Jesse said. "Like what Gabriel did for Michael and Raphael."

The two walked on in silence. Tommy thought about what Jesse had just said and about something God had said earlier. All of a sudden a light bulb popped on in Tommy's head. "I've got an idea!" he exclaimed.

"What is it?" Jesse prompted him, but there was no time for discussion. The gong sounded, signaling Michael's call for the angels to return.

As the group reconvened, Tommy politely waited for his elders to speak first. There were a couple of ideas, but nothing substantial.

During a lull, Michael looked out at the assembled masses and said, "Nothing? Nothing else?"

That is when Tommy, for the second time that day, timidly raised his hand.

"What makes God happy is good works," Tommy said, standing. Everyone nodded at this. "When I met with Him, He said He doubted if we could find five random people who would place the interests of others before themselves. So, why don't we find five people who will do something good? While there may be a lot of bad people in the world, and a lot of people who just don't think, there are also good people who do think. All we need to do is find them. Or encourage them. If we show this to God, maybe then He will feel better."

As Tommy sat, a silence settled over the room that was so profound it seemed to Tommy to last forever. In reality it was only a few moments long, however.

Gabriel broke the silence. "The kid's got something there. The Big Guy is always a sucker for a good-hearted story."

"The Big Guy?" Raphael looked at him askance.

Gabriel just shrugged.

"I like it," Michael spoke emphatically.

Another angel asked if they really thought they could find five people willing to do some random act of kindness.

Still a third wondered how they would go about locating such people and documenting the stories.

Raphael remarked, "It sounds like we are just quibbling over how to accomplish this. I do not detect any disagreement with Tommy's core proposition."

Everyone nodded or murmured his (or her) assent.

Someone said, "The angelic is in the details. The idea may be sound, but getting it accomplished is quite a different matter."

Raphael gently advised the speaker, "It may be difficult, but nothing is impossible. Never has been for us angels."

"It's not hard at all." All eyes turned to Gabriel. "As a matter of fact, I think it is very easy. The time has again come to send another angel into the world. Let him poke around, find five good-hearted people for us to present to the Lord."

Almost everyone was in agreement.

One hard-to-convert cherub asked what if the angel failed to locate five such humans?

"Que sera, será," Gabriel said.

Michael seemed about to protest as he opened his mouth but then apparently reconsidered. "Actually," he said, "Gabe is right. If that happens, we will still be no worse off than we are now."

"Besides," Gabriel added, "if that happens, then we move on to Plan B."

Raphael made a wry face. "Did I miss something? What Plan B?"

Gabriel shrugged. "The one we will come up with if this one fails. Which it won't. Right, Tommy?" The archangel stepped down to give Tommy a high five. Just before he reached Tommy, his arm raised high in the air, Michael called out sharply, "Not now, Gabriel!"

Gabriel halted in his tracks and swatted ferociously at empty air. "Dang mosquitoes!" he said. "You'd think this being Paradise and all, the Big Guy could get rid of the pesky things."

Michael gave him a look that said there was a pesky thing that could be gotten rid of, all right. Gabriel got the message and demurely resumed his seat.

Raphael said, "Gabriel is correct about one thing. We need to follow the power of positive thinking. Plan A is going to work."

Gabriel repeated the phrase, "'the power of positive thinking.' Wasn't that Peale?" referring to the 1950s evangelist Doctor Norman Vincent Peale. Then he got a faux-quizzical look. "Or was it? I always confuse the evangelist Peale with the apostle Paul. Sometimes I find Paul appealing and Peale appalling. And other times…"

There were a few chuckles. Even Michael allowed himself a grin—as did Dr. Peale, who sat up near the front of the room.

Raphael leaned over to Michael and asked which angel would be the designated messenger to visit mankind. "Should we send Gabriel again?"

"Uh-uh," Gabriel said. "I just went to see Mary. I'm exhausted from that trip."

Raphael looked at his brother angel. "Gabriel, that was a long time ago."

"It seems like it was just yesterday."

"It was over two thousand years ago."

Gabriel tapped at his wrist, where he would be wearing a watch if in fact he owned or needed one. "Gosh, I had better get this dang thing fixed. It keeps terrible time."

Michael said, "No, this is not a mission for Gabriel. I think I have the perfect candidate to send…you!" He was looking in Tommy's direction. The little angel looked behind him to see who else Michael could have been referring to.

"Hey, Tommy," Gabriel called out kindly. "He means you."

"M…m…me? But I just got here."

"All the more reason for you to go," Michael said. "Besides, it was your idea.". The archangel looked over the multitude of the heavenly host. "All in favor?"

Millions of wings flapped together.

Michael smiled. "It is unanimous. Tommy, why don't you stay after this session so we can go over the mission details? All right, angels...dismissed!"

Gabriel called out, "Don't forget tonight's harp concert!"

The mass dispersed, mostly by just fading away.

Tommy was trembling slightly. He felt a reassuring pat on his back. "Don't worry," Jesse said. "I'll be right there with you."

They both approached the archangelic triumvirate.

"Nervous?" Raphael smiled in a knowing way.

Tommy nodded.

"A little bit of butterflies is good," Gabriel said. "Michael has a knack for sending the right person at the right time. Besides, we have a great track record."

"You've never failed?" Tommy asked.

"Almost never," Raphael said.

"There was the Nixon administration," Gabriel reminded him.

"All right. So once a millennium we screw up," Raphael retorted.

"Thomas, I have faith in you," Michael said. "You will perform admirably." The archangel's words were very reassuring to Tommy. The little angel stopped trembling and suddenly felt no fear. He shared this bit of news with the small group.

"Excellent," Raphael said. "That is just as it should be. Once an angel receives his or her mission, there is no doubt. Only resolve. And good will."

"But I am not sure what to do. I'm only six."

"Six and three quarters," Gabriel corrected.

It did make Tommy feel bigger.

"Are there special instructions so I know exactly what to do?" the little angel asked.

"No," Raphael said. "If we were to lay it all out for you, then we might as well do it ourselves. The good news is you have freedom to accomplish this as you see fit."

Freedom of action sounded like a good concept, but Tommy still did not have a clue as to how he would go about this. It was as if the other angels read his thoughts, for Raphael said, "First wander the Earth. When you come across someone in whom you perceive goodness, then encourage that person to perform an act based on his or her better nature."

"What sort of act?" Tommy inquired.

"Why, what you suggested at the conclave," Raphael asked. "An act to help others less fortunate than they. There is no shortage of want in the world, is there?"

Tommy had to admit there were plenty of opportunities for charitable works.

"Should I go to a poor country, where people are starving or dying?" the little angel asked.

"Good works do not have to be so grandiose," Michael explained. "Simple acts of kindness, done to just one person, lead to a cascade effect. One good deed begets another. And so on, and so on."

"Until you have a world of good cheer," Raphael concluded.

"The other thing is we would not send you into a less developed country on your very first time out," Michael added. "Past experience has shown that it is better for you to cut your teeth, so to speak, somewhere closer to home. Somewhere where you will be very comfortable in your surroundings."

That made sense to Tommy. He looked at Jesse, who smiled reassuringly.

"So?" Raphael asked. "Are you in?"

Tommy again looked at Jesse's encouraging features and, turning back to the archangels, said, "Yes sir, uh sirs. I will do it!"

The triumvirate smiled.

"When do I start?" Tommy next asked. He figured it would take months for him to finish his angelic basic training. Then he would be prepared to tackle this project.

"There is no time like the present," Michael proclaimed. "You start...right now!"

Tommy made a sound that in human terms could only have been a gulp.

"First, however," Michael told him, "we have to go over the rules."

"Yes," Raphael somberly intoned. "The rules."

"Too many infernal rules," Gabriel muttered. "You take an easy concept, flap your wings and do good, and we clutter it up with a whole bunch of rules." After a look from Michael and Raphael he quickly amended his thought, adding, "Which of course are quite important."

"Why don't you have a seat and make yourself comfortable," Michael invited Tommy. "You, too, Jesse, though you have had the benefit of this lecture before."

Tommy looked around, then at the sitting angels. There was nary a chair in sight. He shrugged and simply fell backward... onto a bit of cloud that had strategically placed itself at the last moment. One had appeared for Jesse as well.

Tommy looked up at Michael and his cohort, wondering what would follow. What exactly did they mean by the rules?

"Rule number one," Raphael said. "You have a short time frame for accomplishing your mission. Down there it is the day before the day before Christmas."

"Christmas Eve Eve," Gabriel commented. "Or Christmas Eve squared."

Raphael ignored him. "You have only two Earth days before you must return, regardless of what you are in the middle of. By the stroke of midnight heralding in Christmas day, or sooner if we call you back, you must return. This rule is inviolate."

Tommy asked if that was because he had to be on hand for the heavenly celebration, also fortuitously set for Christmas Day.

Raphael told him that was not the case. "Other angels will miss the festivities, their duties taking them out of our realm." Instead, he told the little angel, it was a matter of restricting time spent back in the world.

Tommy was confused. "But I thought there is no time in heaven?"

"There isn't," Raphael agreed. "You have just come from Earth, however. We cannot afford to have you, or any angel for that matter, become re-attached to the land of the living. Hence the two-day limit."

Tommy could understand the logic in that. "But it does not give me much time for the job."

Raphael conceded it did not. "However," he said, "you must remember we are angels. We have abilities that allow us to cram a lot more into a moment than any human can do. To do that you will have to start thinking like an angel, not like a boy."

"How do I do that?"

"It is part of your mission. You will figure it out."

Tommy swallowed, letting his personal doubts in his abilities go unvoiced.

Next Gabriel spoke. "The second rule. If you ever come face to face with the Evil One, run as fast as you can."

Tommy smiled, figuring Gabriel was being humorous. "You're kidding, right?"

But Gabriel's face was serious—very serious. "Lucifer is the one thing I never, never joke about," the archangel said. "It is complicated, but fortunately we sealed him off in his chasm so he can never enter here for all eternity. But there is a porthole through which he can visit Earth from time to time. He is the epitome of hate. A liar and the father of all lies. He exists solely to thwart our good works. If he senses your mission, he will stop at nothing to drag you under."

That sounded intimidating to Tommy, but the idea of flight in the face of evil surprised him. "Why should I run?" he asked. "Why not fight him?"

"Because you cannot win," Gabriel said. "Not by fighting. That is what Satan wants. For you to become consumed with hatred of him and to fight. His everlasting weakness is love. You defeat him by turning the other cheek."

"But you fought him."

Gabriel nodded, still solemn. "Yes," he said, "but it is not in the sort of battle you envision. We defeated him with love."

"I'm not sure I understand," Tommy said, to which Gabriel told him it was a difficult concept. One they would open his mind to, albeit at a later time.

"You must promise me, Tommy," Gabriel said. "If you see him, run."

The archangel looked searchingly at the newest angel.

"All right. I promise," Tommy told Gabriel and the others. "But what does he look like?"

"That is part of his deceit," Gabriel responded. "He changes his appearance to fit whatever temptation is appropriate. He could be a horrible demon, a seductive temptress, a little old lady, a pleasant-looking businessman. You name it. It is like what the humans say about pornography. You will know it when you see it."

Tommy wrinkled his nose. "What's 'nography?"

"You are so young," Gabriel said with a sigh.

"Dirty pictures," Jesse whispered in his ear.

"Oh, I get it."

Next Michael spoke. "The third rule," he said, "is the most serious of all. It is the only one that can get you expelled from the heavenly host. Under no condition must you ever, ever reveal your true identity to people who knew you on Earth without direct authorization from the Lord."

Tommy shrugged. "That doesn't sound so tough."

"When you are on Earth, you must become as one of them," Michael continued.

Tommy said he believed he could do that.

Michael nodded and then added, "In the conclave, when you raised your hand, you said there were two items you wanted to discuss. The first of course was the matter of God's disappointment with the world. You never got around to the second, Tommy. It is about your parents, isn't it?"

Tommy stared at the archangel. "Can angels read minds?" he asked.

Michael smiled. "No. But we do intercept prayers. Even here your concern for your mother and father is in your silent prayers—and we have heard it." Raphael and Gabriel nodded. "It is true your parents are very sad right now," Michael continued. "That is common when a loved one dies, and that it is exacerbated when the loved one is a child, like you were."

"Is there anything we can do to ease their sadness?" Tommy pleaded.

Michael nodded. "Every angel is allowed to share one vision with someone back on Earth. Almost every angel uses their gift to let their loved ones know they are all right. That seems to ease the survivor's distress. You do not have to use it in that way, however. You are free to share the gift however you deem fit."

"Oh, that would be wonderful!" Tommy exclaimed.

Michael told him that was primarily why he was sending the little angel on this mission. It would allow Tommy to assuage both God's sorrow and Tommy's parents' grief at the same time.

"Oh, thank you! Thank you!" Tommy said, overjoyed.

"But remember," Michael added, "only one vision may be shared. There are no others and no appeal to this. And it must be done in a way that does not compromise your angelic nature and identity before your loved ones. As I noted, that rule is inviolable."

Thus far Tommy had been happy in heaven, but now he was really on cloud nine, for his parents' sake. The little angel grinned from ear to ear.

"We will see you in two human days' time," Raphael told him. "If you are successful, you will earn your angel's wings."

Tommy was still grinning. "When I do, is it true that a bell rings?"

"Oh, don't go all Hollywood on us, kid," Gabriel said.

"Before you take your leave," Michael said, "we have to do something about your appearance."

Tommy frowned. "You mean, like washing behind my ears?"

Michael said that was not what he meant. Tommy's appearance had to be altered for two reasons. One, to cloak his true identity, apropos of the previously invoked rule. The second was that humans tended not to take children seriously.

Michael stretched out his arm—and Tommy was transformed. Tommy could feel it. Somehow he was larger, much larger. There were no mirrors in heaven. There had never been a need for them. Gabriel held out his hands, forming them into a frame. Suddenly it was as if a mirror appeared inside the archangel's hands! Tommy gazed at his reflection. He was bigger. In fact he was all grown up!

The not-so-little angel looked questioningly at the three archangels. Then Raphael said, "This is what you would have looked like as an adult."

Tommy rubbed at his face. His cheeks felt rough. Whiskery. It was strange.

"This is a good age to send you down at," Raphael said.

"How old am I? I mean, in this body?"

"Thirty-three," Raphael answered. "In cases like this we always make the angel thirty-three."

Tommy wrinkled his nose another time. "Why thirty-three? Why not twenty-three? Or some really old age, like forty-three?"

Michael said, "The Lord is partial to that age."

Tommy thought for only a second and of course got it. "That was Jesus' age…" He let the thought trail off.

"Jesse will give you a few last-minute ideas," Michael said. "Good luck." And he vanished.

"Bon voyage!" Raphael said as he too vanished. "Have a fulfilling trip," came his voice from beyond the void.

"Don't forget to write," Gabriel said as a hand reached out from the nothing and pulled the last archangel away also.

"Nervous?" Jesse asked. They were the only ones left.

"Uh-huh."

"Don't be. You have a lot going for you, especially with the angelic powers. Here, let me give you a few pointers. And of course in case of trouble, don't forget to call." Jesse then went over a number of practical things Tommy would have to know. He also told Tommy that as time went on, his angel powers would develop. When he was done he embraced Tommy. "You will do fine," he said, smiling. Then he too vanished.

Tommy looked around. "Here goes nothing," he said. Then he stepped off the cloud as Jesse had instructed him.

✦Two✦

As he walked, the brightness of heaven faded and faded, and other objects began to form before him, very dimly at first. With each step the forms took on more substance. After Tommy had gone a half dozen paces he stumbled a bit, almost as if he had stubbed the toe of his shoe on some uneven pavement or something. In wonder he looked around at the familiar trees and buildings and the few pedestrians. Then up to the sky. The moon was full and equally familiar, as were the constellations. Tommy smiled and let out his breath, which he could see in the chill night air. He was back on Earth.

Even though so much was familiar, the surroundings did not quite match anything from Tommy's hometown. He looked about but could see no signs or distinguishing landmarks. At this late hour and given the cold winter weather, there were few fellow travelers, and all were bundled up and walking quickly. Tommy was not about to ask any of them where he was. It would only call attention to his status as a stranger. There were some bright lights in the distance. Tommy put his hands in his coat pockets and walked toward them, hoping to find a shopping mall or a plaza. Perhaps there he would find out precisely where he had landed.

It was a short walk. Tommy could have flown, but the risk of detection was too great, and he was uncertain of his angel-sense of direction, so he walked. Sure enough, he soon reached a strip mall. And a bus stop with a newspaper stand. Of course there had been no money in heaven. Tommy looked one way, then the other, to be sure he was not being observed. Then he wiggled his finger and the paper slot popped open. Tommy withdrew a paper and looked at it carefully. The heading on the paper was emblazoned: "The *Journal-News*—Rockland's Hometown Newspaper." There was a silhouette of the state (New York) and a tiny X denoting the region the paper served. Tommy had an idea what had happened. He carefully put the paper back and resumed walking.

"Nanuet Auto," "Buy-Rite—Best Liquor Store in Nanuet," "First National Bank of Nanuet." No doubt he was in a town called Nanuet, in Rockland County, New York. In the far distance Tommy saw a major highway. Using his angel vision he read the signs closely. "Thruway North—Albany—120 miles." That was near to where Tommy had lived.

Tommy exhaled deeply. Jesse had said new angels frequently missed the mark the first few times out. Tommy now saw he had overshot his goal by about 150 miles. At least he had hit the right state.

His original plan had been to head first to his old hometown and search out his parents (though they would not know him) and share a comforting vision with them. Tommy even had decided on the vision he would show them. It would be of him in heaven, happy in the hereafter. Mom and Dad were regular churchgoers and had faith, but he knew a jolt such as they had received could cause doubt to creep in. Nothing could bring Tommy back, but once they were made to realize he was safe in the heavenly abode, Tommy was sure their grief would dissipate.

He did not want to take angel steps to get to his parents, however. Jesse had warned him that if his sense of direction was off, it would be fruitless to continue trying to hit the landing zone. Most likely he would keep under- or over-shooting the spot. Jesse said he might spend more time in a series of heavenly hops than if he simply resorted to human means of travel. Given that time was a factor, Tommy decided Jesse was right. But he did not have any money for a bus. Certainly he did not have wheels, and it was too far to walk. Tommy figured he would hitch a ride. Perhaps that would be the first act of kindness he could coax out of a stranger. So he set off in the direction of the highway.

Tommy had not walked far when he heard—something. Stopping in his tracks, he listened carefully. What came through was garbled at first, like a bad transmission over radio waves. Lots of static and multiple voices. The more Tommy concentrated, the clearer it became. Tommy looked to his left. About twenty feet away another pedestrian was walking her dog. Neither dog walker nor dog could hear the voice, however. Because the voice was not of this world. It was something only angels and saints could hear—a prayer. Like so many silent prayers, this one was not grandly composed like the "Our Father." Nor was it a less poetic but still strictly verbal recitation. It was a primal scream for help. The reason Tommy did not pick up the complete chatter, but only a distorted voice, was that his angel sense was not yet fully matured. Nor had his directional beacon improved yet, for he could not discern where the prayer was coming from. There were only two likely sources. A nearby neighborhood, likely the one the dog and its owner hailed from, and a church.

Tommy's first impulse was to head over to the cluster of houses and see if someone was in serious need of assistance. As he took his first tentative steps toward the neighborhood, his ears detected the faint notes of a familiar melody. One of the houses in the neighborhood was all decked out for the Christmas season, and it emitted enough wattage to be seen from Saturn. Its yard was full of enough plastic to put a major dent in the world strategic plastic reserve. Santas, a Winnie-the-Pooh with Saint Nicholas's sack, hordes of reindeer, barnyard animals, an elf display, giant candy canes, mock presents and gingerbread people were assembled everywhere. It was the type of house that was so turned out cars from near and far would ride past for a glimpse of what passed in this world as some people's idea of Christmas cheer. None of that was what had attracted Tommy's seventh (heavenly) sense. What he did notice was the music pouring forth from the speakers set high on the roof, camouflaged behind the reindeer heads. It was the Christmas carol that had always been one of Tommy's favorites. *Silent Night.*

As he paused to enjoy the carol, Tommy's eyes strayed involuntarily to the church nearby. Deciding, though not consciously so, that he was meant to go there, Tommy shifted direction and headed for God's house.

The church was only dimly lit, but even with limited wattage the stained glass window in front mesmerized Tommy. Moreso than all the plastic figures in the yard a few yards away, which really did not properly commemorate God's birth.

Tommy reasoned the inside light meant the building must be open. He had heard there was a time when church doors remained open twenty-four hours a day. Now, however, as befitted the times, the doors were barred at sundown. Why, Tommy had even heard that the way into Saint Peter's in Rome was barred by a chain. How sad! No wonder God was depressed by what His creation had become.

Sure enough, Tommy's instincts were spot on. The church door did open. A bulletin at the entrance told him this place was dedicated to Saint Anthony of Padua. Tommy smiled. That was one saint he would make a point of looking up when he returned. Inside it was quiet, save for a votive candle on the major altar that made quiet but distinctive crackling sounds. Tommy had half hoped there would be a choir getting ready for midnight Mass. He so would have enjoyed listening to some Christmas carols. The religious kind, not the ones about snowmen, santas and reindeer, but about Jesus, Mary and Joseph.

The only person inside was a middle-aged man slumped on a kneeler in the front pew. His shoulders were heaving, and the occasional sob could be heard clear to the back where Tommy stood due to the wonderful acoustics. The little angel in the grown-up body looked about and took in the grandeur of this holy place. Even without the poinsettias, garland and holly, the building had a majesty of its own.

Tommy shuffled slowly up the main aisle to the weeping, uncomprehending figure. When he was close he intentionally made a noise, letting his hand rap along the wooden pew, so as not to scare the poor creature half to death.

Even at that, the man did jump slightly from his kneeling position. "Oh! You startled me!"

"I did not mean to," Tommy said as he studied the man's grief-contorted features. Despite the sorrow etched in that face Tommy perceived a kindliness in the fiftyish man. He wore a Roman collar. The man quickly wiped at his eyes and averted his face as though hoping to keep his inner tragedy hidden. With a hastily produced handkerchief he wiped at his nose. Composed, though only barely, the man asked if he could help Tommy.

"Perhaps it is *I* who can help *you*," Tommy quietly suggested. He quickly added, "You are a priest?"

The man shook his head and held out his hand but emitted another strong sniffle that he struggled somewhat unsuccessfully to get under control. "I am a deacon. Deacon John Cutter. Deacon John, the parishioners call me. You're new here."

"Just passing through."

"And you are?"

"Thomas. Tommy to my friends."

Deacon John looked Tommy up and down. "Tommy…last name?"

Tommy did not think angels were supposed to lie and he did not see the harm, so he gave his actual last name.

"What brings you to Nanuet, Tommy? Not too many people come through here unless they are visiting family. Are you on your way to visit family for Christmas?"

"No, sir. As much as I wish it, my, er, business will keep me away from my family this Christmas."

"They from around here?"

"'Bout one hundred fifty miles north and a little west. A small town called Colonie. It's near Albany, on the way to Cooperstown."

"Ah," John said, smiling at last. "I know Cooperstown well, and of course I have been to the Hall of Fame."

Leave it to baseball to bring a smile to any red-blooded American male, Tommy thought, no matter how sad he might have been just a moment before.

"Yessir," Tommy said. "I used to love going to the museum with Dad." He spoke a little wistfully.

"Well, my son," John said, "business or no business, it's not all that far away. You really ought to get up there, at least on Christmas Day, to be with your folks."

Tommy shrugged. "Not possible, much as I wish."

The deacon asked if Tommy needed money for bus fare. Tommy assured him that was not the impediment. Then he turned the conversation. "What about you, Deacon? You seemed mighty sad when I entered the church."

The deacon shrugged. "Nothing I can't handle. We all have our crosses to bear from time to time. We just have to work through the rough patches."

"Probably easier for you, being armed with God."

To which the deacon made a derisive snort somewhat involuntarily.

Tommy looked at him questioningly.

"I'm sorry," John said. "I don't mean to mislead you. You see, this is my last night in the Church. I am planning on leaving the deaconate."

This admission seemed to pain the deacon.

"But why?" Tommy asked.

Deacon John got a vacant look in his eyes as he sat in the pew. Tommy took the seat next to him. The cleric spoke in a very tiny voice. "I...I am afraid...I have lost my faith." He smirked. "Can't be much of a religious without faith."

"Surely you do not doubt God's existence?" Tommy said.

John shrugged. "Who knows?"

"Did something bad happen?" Tommy probed. "Church politics or something?" In his brief time in heaven he had heard stories of men of the cloth frustrated by the worldly affairs of organized religious bureaucracy.

"No. No." Deacon John waved him off. "Nothing like that."

Tommy just stared wonderingly.

"It's a long story."

"I'm a good listener," Tommy assured the troubled cleric.

Deacon John sighed deeply as he began to tell his tale. At first Tommy had to strain to hear him, but as John went along his voice, while still timid, grew stronger.

"I was not always a man of the cloth," he said, "though from my earliest days I believed I would be. Just after college, I went to Fordham, a Jesuit institution, and felt I had the calling. So upon graduation I entered the seminary. In my second year at the sem, we were sent off on a mission to Appalachia to work alongside a group of people from Habitat for Humanity.

"There I met a girl. She was a social worker from the Bronx. Her name was Holly, because she had been a Christmas baby." John looked up at nothing in particular, seeing a memory that was visible only to him. Tommy could see the deacon's eyes were again moist. "Funny," John said. "I never believed in love at first sight until that moment. I spent the weekend with her. How could I not? We were in close quarters, rebuilding a school in eastern Kentucky. When I got back to Dunwoodie (which was the seminary), I tried to force all thoughts of Holly out of my mind. I prayed with a vengeance...I mean that in a good way," he said with half a smile. "I put my body through so many penances to force anything worldly out of my mind, it was ridiculous. But nothing worked. I went to my confessor, who said as much as they'd love to have me, a half-committed priest was worse than no priest at all. He told me to leave Dunwoodie... take a leave of absence...to explore my true feelings for Holly. The Holy Spirit would reveal the correct path, either to Holly or back to the sem.

"The second I saw Holly the first night after leaving Dunwoodie, it was like nothing I had ever imagined. I knew right away. The funny thing is she was the nervous one because she did not want to stand in the way of my vocation. I had to convince her. They say absence makes the heart grow fonder. Must be true. Two days later I asked Holly to marry me. Thank God, she said yes.

"Two years after we were married, she died in a car accident."

Tommy winced. "That must have been horrible!"

John nodded. "It was...it was. But I had two things to get me through. My faith. And Clare. You see, Holly and I had a baby the year before. So for Clare's sake I had to soldier on."

"Clare is a pretty name," Tommy said.

John nodded again. "I had always been partial to Saint Francis of Assisi. It was Holly's idea to name the baby Clare." He did not have to explain that Clare was the twelfth-century associate of Francis who founded the order of Poor Clares.

"She's a remarkable person. Clare."

"My Clare? Or Saint Clare?" John said absently.

Without thinking it through, Tommy replied, "Both."

John gave Tommy a strange look but went on. "I had followed Holly into social work. It seemed a fitting occupation given my earlier priestly inclination. After Holly's death I did that for a living and raised Clare."

Tommy asked how long ago this was. From the tone of the conversation, he did not think it was the loss of John's wife that was causing the deacon's crisis of faith. The little angel also sensed more of the story, but he waited for the deacon to narrate it. John then told him the tragedy had occurred twenty years ago.

"You never remarried?" Tommy said this as half question, half statement.

"No. Holly was the only one for me. I used to think until eternity. Now, however, I'm not sure. Oh, I am still sure of my love for her. That will never die, but as to whether she will be waiting for me when I die..." The deacon just shook his head sadly.

"So what happened?" Tommy asked. "It's about Clare, isn't it?"

"Yes. She was a wonderful person, just like her mother. Gave so much meaning to my life. Once Clare was all grown up and had graduated college, I figured my parenting days were over, so I went back and finished my religious training and was ordained a deacon last year. Sort of going back to my original game plan.

"About eight months ago, Clare started having problems with her hearing, then her balance and her memory. The doctors found a brain tumor. It was malignant. They gave her less than a year. But she did not get even close to that. When about five months of that period were up, just a few months ago now, she had a serious incident and was rushed back to the hospital. She was living near Albany. A little town called Colonie. Oh, but you know where Colonie is."

Tommy nodded. Obviously he knew where it was.

"Of course I visited her. Clare told me she could deal with what was happening. She was more concerned that I be all right. She only had one request for herself. When the end came, she asked that I be there, to hold her hand and help deliver her to the hereafter. I told the doctors and the nurses to call me, no matter what, gave them my home, work and cell numbers. They were to call me when the end was near. They figured she still had a few weeks."

John shook his head. Tommy could not tell if he was doing this in anger or pain. "She didn't have weeks as it turned out. Just three days after I last saw her, she took a sudden turn for the worse. Slipped into a coma. All her vital signs were down.

"The hospital called, but I did not take the call right away. You see, I was in the rectory. It was my night to be on duty. A young couple had come in. Nice people. They had three kids. However, a lot of problems had cropped up and they were headed to a divorce. Said I was their last stop before seeing their respective attorneys.

"I was in the midst of counseling them when I heard my cell phone vibrate. I saw it was the hospital number, but I just let it vibrate. I could not leave that couple in mid-discussion. I probably spent, I don't know, another forty-five minutes with them. Then returned the call. When I heard how bad it was, I raced to Albany to the hospital. I was going twenty miles over the speed limit and fortunately no cops were in sight. Got to Albany in record time, less than an hour and a half. It's a straight shot up the Thruway. I prayed the whole way, asking God to please, *please*, keep Clare alive until I arrived. But when I got to the nurses' station..." Here his voice trailed off and he started to choke up.

"When I got there, they told me Clare was gone. It happened a half hour earlier." Now his tears were coming full force. "The one time my baby needed me...the only thing I could do for her...and I...was...not...there...for...her." He buried his face in his hands and cried. Tommy patted his shoulder.

When the deacon had calmed himself a little he said, "Since then there's been a voice inside me that keeps telling me there cannot be a God to allow such a thing to happen. All I've ever done is try to live a good life, help others, and the one time...the one time I needed Him, there was no God there for me." And he wept anew.

Tommy tried to console the poor man. Talked about the new life Clare was enjoying. No matter how hard Tommy tried, however, Deacon John was having none of it.

"I've told myself all that same crap! It's what I have used to console countless parishioners. But, you know, I just don't think I believe anymore. No matter how hard I have tried, that voice keeps coming back to me."

"Your voice?"

Deacon John looked up in surprise. "Funny you should ask that. No. No, it is not my voice. It's a very pleasant voice, like the narrator in a commercial or something. I guess it's just like a dream, or a daydream. But it is very real to me."

Tommy frowned as he tried to make sense of it all. He asked the deacon if his leaving the ministry is what Holly or Clare would have wanted.

"Oh, who knows? Who knows if there is even a Holly or Clare anymore? What if when you die...well, that's just it! There's nothing. No God, no heaven. Nothing!"

"That does not sound like you talking," Tommy went out on a small limb. "That's the voice telling you that."

John nodded.

Tommy said, "I would not be surprised if that voice you hear is from the devil."

The deacon began to protest, but Tommy cut him off. "He is very cunning, you know. To turn a man of God like yourself would be a great coup for the Evil One."

John nodded, indicating that reasoning made sense to him.

Tommy asked if there was a coffee shop nearby where they could get some hot chocolate and continue talking. John nodded again and led the way out of the church. As soon as they stepped outside, a vicious wind howled in a decidedly unearthly manner. A dark cloud raced out of nowhere, stopping just feet from Tommy's face. Tommy was struck by the fact that the deacon was oblivious to this occurrence. Only Tommy saw the cloud. Except it was not a cloud. The formation coalesced, transforming itself into something much different…a face! As horrible a visage as Tommy had ever imagined. The very sight of the awful apparition caused Tommy's knees to shake. The monster-thing laughed, and spittle dripped from its jaws. "You will not win!" it hissed at Tommy. "He is mine! And soon you will be too!"

As they had left the church, out of habit Tommy had dipped his fingers into the holy water font. He now flung his hand in the direction of the spirit, telling it to go away. As Tommy did so, an errant drop of water flew off the tips of his fingers into the cloud. With another fearsome screech and a roar the face made a grimace of intense pain and raced off. In its wake a wind kicked up, hurling pebbles and detritus at Tommy and the deacon.

"Come on!" Tommy cried, practically hauling John back into the church. He had borne in mind the admonition to run if ever confronted by the angel of darkness, and Tommy knew they were safe back inside the church. Satan could not abide even a moment in any place filled with holiness.

Deacon John had remained unaware of all but the final pelting of the wind. "Must have been a dirt devil," he said with a shiver once they were back inside.

"For sure," Tommy said, though with a different meaning of their tormentor in mind.

"All right," Tommy said as he calmed himself. "How do we go about convincing you that leaving is a big mistake?"

Deacon John shook his head sadly. "I don't think you can. There's a 6 A.M. bus to Florida. My plan is to spend the night here in quiet contemplation and, if nothing changes my mind, get on that bus. Enjoy some warmth in the sunny south and start my new life, whatever that will be."

"But think of all the people you will be leaving behind," Tommy protested.

Deacon John snorted. "The people. Hah! Who knows if I've had an impact on them!"

Tommy shook his head. He perceived so much goodness in this man that he knew John had to be a wonderful servant of the Lord. That was when Tommy had his epiphany. He would find parishioners whose lives John had touched to personally bear witness to the deacon's good works. That should turn the evil voices aside.

Tommy told John he had an errand to run and asked the deacon to wait for him. "I'll be back!"

To the little angel's rapidly retreating back John called out, "As long as you're back before six in the morning. 'Cause I'll be long gone by then."

The first place Tommy sought help was the one which to his mind was the most logical. The church rectory. Why not enlist the aid of one of the priests? The rectory was a small building next to the church. Tommy rang the bell. Actually, it was a buzzer. Nothing happened. Tommy pushed it again. Then a third time.

At last Tommy heard stirring on the other side of the door. Probably the stairs creaking. "I'm comin'! I'm comin'!" a voice growled.

The door was flung open and a white-haired old man, eyes ablaze and nostrils flaring, yelled, "Do you know what time it is?"

"I need a priest!" Tommy implored.

"That would be me. That's why I was asleep. I have the 9 A.M. daily Mass tomorrow!" The elderly priest did not introduce himself. It also did not seem unduly burdensome to Tommy to have to wake up for a nine o'clock Mass. He held his tongue, however. What he did say was, "It's about Deacon John. We need to help him."

"Is he hurt?" the priest grumbled.

"Not physically."

"What other kind is there?"

"Spiritual."

"Oh, for the love of…are you a feckin' bishop or something? Don't pester me at all hours of the night about your stupid spiritual concerns!"

"Isn't that what a priest's job is all about?" Tommy asked innocently enough.

The priest started to shut the door, but Tommy held it open with his foot. "If you have trouble getting back to sleep, may I suggest a little reading?" Tommy said in a mock polite tone. "How about the parable of the Good Samaritan? The part about the priest who could not be bothered to help his fellow man."

Then Tommy retracted his foot. The priest glared again, unleashed a quite unpriestly epithet and growled, "I see we have a theologian here!" as he slammed the door.

"Well, we certainly don't have a theologian there," Tommy spoke to the closed door.

Tommy wondered how much time had elapsed.

In heaven time was not a constraint, but Tommy knew down here in the world time mattered. Glancing at the church's clock tower he saw that it was almost eleven o'clock. Where would he find parishioners before the world took to their beds? "Think. Think. Think," he said, imitating one of his favorite storybook characters, Winnie-the-Pooh. Even Tommy realized in some ways he was still a child despite his new life and the angelic wisdom that had already been imparted to him.

A screech of tires forced Tommy's attention to a rapidly re-treating car. Through its rear window Tommy saw a passel of packages. "Of course!" he snapped his fingers. This made him doubly pleased, because while a child Tommy had not yet been able to learn how to snap his fingers. Or to whistle. He tried to whistle now and was again pleased at the pleasant sounds he was able to make. These were fleeting thoughts, however, because of Tommy's realization that, at this time of year, stores were open late. Until midnight, Tommy guessed. So he hurried to the nearby mall. Sure enough it was open. Not as crowded this near to closing time as it undoubtedly had been during prime time, but there were enough cars to give Tommy hope.

Tommy willed himself to walk, talk and act in a calm fashion. His mouth dropped open, however, when he entered the main doors of the mall. People were hustling, a few were actually in full jog (many were too obese to sprint) from store to store. Most were laden with packages. He saw a few totally graceless people, literally pushing others out of their way.

Unbidden, the words of the Apostle's Creed popped into Tommy's head, the part where it said, "He descended into hell."

Taking a deep breath, Tommy waded into the fast-moving stream of greed and approached the first person he saw, a middle-aged man holding two packages and fairly running into a store where he could purchase his third. Tommy broke into a trot to keep up with the man. "Excuse me, sir," he said. "Do you go to Saint Anthony's?"

"Out of my way, dumb-ass. I'm busy."

Tommy was taken aback by the rudeness and did not even attempt a reply—or a second effort.

The next person in his line of sight was a woman. "Excuse me," Tommy said. He again found himself triple-timing his strides to keep up. "I'm trying to help Deacon John at Saint Anthony's and…"

"Beat it, creep-o. That is the lamest pick-up line I've ever heard."

So it went. Tommy was variously told to get lost, where to stick it, threatened to have the cops sicked on him. Other typical responses were "Bizzeegottagooo," "Freakin' Jesus freak," words that should not be dignified in print, and no response at all. Those who made no response just clamped down on their jaws, got a serious look like they were about to advise the president on the unemployment problem and scooted off—with nary a word.

Then there was one who said, "I gave already."

"I'm not collecting," Tommy replied.

"Doesn't matter. I gave already."

Tommy was about to seek his next target for charity when the loudspeaker announced that the mall was now closed until eight the next morning. Tommy was standing near one of the exits, and his eyes grew wide as saucers as he saw what could have been the cast of *Ben Hur* stream toward him. Well, actually toward the exit, but inasmuch as Tommy was the only thing standing between the throng and bedtime, he flung himself to the side to avoid getting trampled to death. Except that he could not be trampled to death. He was already dead.

Then Tommy saw a rarity: a bank of pay phones. He'd heard about pay phones from his parents, who'd joked once that they'd gone the way of rotary dial phones, whatever those were. But the Nanuet Mall still had pay phones, and they had given Tommy an idea. He would call the couple Deacon John had helped. Perhaps they could be coaxed to repay the favor. In his recitation of his story, John had mentioned the family's name. Using his newfound angel sense, Tommy lifted a receiver of one of the phones. He had neither change nor a directory listing, but he had something better: angelpower. Gripping the receiver, he willed it to ring at the other end.

On the fourth ring someone answered. Tommy began in rapid cadence, "Mr. and Mrs. Pierce, you do not know me, but I am calling because of Deacon John. He needs your help…"

Tommy was forced to stop because there was no one on the other end. Just a pronounced beep, followed by, "This is the Pierce residence. We are unable to take your call at this time, but please leave your name, number and a brief message and we will return your call as soon as we can." Followed by another loud and prolonged beep.

Tommy left a brief message to the effect that a mutual friend, Deacon John, needed help and could they please call. As for his number, Tommy shrugged and said to call 432-8367. He thought to actually pay a personal visit at the Pierce's residence but discarded the idea, because they were either truly not at home or were likely asleep. Having seen how grouchy the old priest had become when awakened from hibernation, Tommy did not relish a replay of that.

Outside, Tommy tried to flag down a few of the motorists, but not only did no one stop, Tommy was fortunate not to have one run him over. The exodus from the parking area was the epitome of road rage. It all happened so fast. A lot of horns honking, clouds of carbon monoxide, tons of extended middle fingers and then all was calm and bright.

Tommy turned and saw an unkempt man leaning against one of the columns supporting the portico at the mall's entrance. The man was rail thin, so much so that Tommy guessed he was ill. He had noticeable stubble and bloodshot eyes and his hair was askew. Next to the man was a Mets cap, which now lay on the ground upturned. There was some loose change and a dollar bill in the cap.

"Some people, huh?" the man asked Tommy as he approached. "I saw you trying to flag one down. Fuhgeddaboutit."

"Well," Tommy said companionably, "I figured with Christmas and all…"

The man cut him off. "You know what feast we are celebratin'?"

"Sure," Tommy answered brightly. "Christmas. The Incarnation."

"Nah. Not the Incarnation. It's the Self-Absorption. That's what it brings out in people. If you think otherwise, look at my haul." He indicated the hat. "A dollah thirty-seven. The bill in there is mine. I put it in to prime the pump, so to speak. Ya' know, I read this is the eighth-richest county in the United States, and the best they could donate at Christmas time is a buck thirty-seven. It sucks."

Tommy asked what cause the man was collecting for.

"I lost my job eight months ago. Haven't been able to get any work, what with this damn recession an' all. I've got three kids. I just wanted to scrape together enough to get somethin' small for 'em for Christmas." He snorted at the handful of change in his overturned cap. "What'm I gonna' get 'em with this? A pack of chewing gum?"

He finally stooped down and picked up the cap, carefully putting the money, little as it was, in his threadbare pocket.

Tommy suggested the man might try harder to find work. Even if the job market was lagging, surely there were jobs somewhere so he would not have to resort to begging.

"Pah! You don't think I've tried? Applied to everything from the pizza parlor up the road a ways, to landscapers, all sorts of businesses. They all say the same thing. Times are rough. We've had to let people go. Not hirin' now." His eyes grew wide as he exclaimed, "And don't talk to me about any of that Christmas crap!"

Tommy had just begun to wonder where the poor soul's guardian angel was at. Now he realized. Guardian angels are tremendous allies to have around, but they are especially susceptible to rejection. That is, you have to be open to them. And this poor fellow certainly was not spiritually open.

Then the man told Tommy, "You seem like a nice person. Would you give me somethin'?" He held out his hand as if grasping at a lifeline.

Tommy told him he had no money. "But what I have, in the name of the Lord of all, I give you," and he extended his hands over the poor man's head.

The man looked out of the corner of his eyes. "What the heck're you doin'?"

Tommy shrugged, for it seemed obvious. "I'm blessing you."

"I can't eat a damn blessing."

Tommy turned to go. No wonder the guardian angel had left this guy.

Something in Tommy's hurt look must have touched the man, however. He called out to Tommy and shuffled rapidly after the little angel. "That was mean of me. Who can't use a blessing now and then? Go ahead, man. Give me your blessing. Can't hurt, can it?"

Tommy smiled and once again extended his hands and prayed for the man's soul. The fellow was named Edward. It was a silent prayer. Tommy had been instructed those were the best kind. Better than the crass and showy prayers of those who seemed to find it necessary to flap their gums and their arms all about when they prayed. To them the reward was in the recognition, not the blessing, which debased the prayer itself.

Edward asked Tommy if he wanted to join him for a snack.

"But I thought..."

Now Edward waved his arm. "I mean I'm gonna' check out the trash bins. Lotsa' times there's good stuff people throw away."

"Come on," Tommy said, grabbing Edward's arm and pulling him along.

"Where we goin'? You're not a cop, are you? You're not gonna' hurt me?" There was genuine fear in Edward's voice.

Tommy calmed him. "I would never do anything to hurt you. I just blessed you, didn't I?" The problem was, Edward did not know his benefactor of the moment was a real angel, and angel blessings are something special. "Let's find you a job," Tommy insisted.

"At this hour?"

"Listen," Tommy told him. "The mall only just closed. So the office should still be open. Tell me, what talent do you have?"

"I'm real good with my hands."

Tommy looked at him in a new light. "You mean, like a carpenter."

"Yeah. I guess so."

"Like Jesus."

Edward grinned. "If'n I could turn water into wine, we'd really be cookin'."

"Oh ye of little faith."

Inside the mall they took the elevator to the top floor, where the management office was. Edward said, "You are one of the craziest cats I ever come across, but what does it say about me? I'm the one followin' you."

Tommy laughed and said, "That's probably what Peter and a bunch of the other fishermen said the first time they took after Jesus."

They got out of the elevator on the fourth floor, where a harried-looking gentleman with thinning hair and tie askew was locking his office.

"Excuse me, sir. We are looking for building management," Tommy said pleasantly enough.

"That's me. We're closed now. Come back in the morning." The man's tone was gruff. Not as in my-voice-is-usually-gruff sounding, but more like I-am-not-in-a-friendly-mood gruff. Edward would have turned back right away, but Tommy persevered as if he were totally tone deaf to the speaker's voice.

"Well, we won't keep you, sir, and in fact we can walk along with you as we talk. This fellow here, his name is Edward and he has above-average carpentry skills." The mall manager glowered and Edward managed a weak smile.

The man took off briskly for the stairs. Nonplussed, Tommy stayed in tow. Edward reluctantly padded along. "So," Tommy implored, "what can we do for Edward?"

"What do you mean *we*, kemo sabe? Don't you read the papers, guy?" the manager growled. "There's a recession going on."

"More important than that," Tommy pointed out, still in his very agreeable tone, "the papers also note that it is Christmas."

The man shook his head. "Jesus Christ."

Tommy brightened. "Exactly."

The man thought he had misheard. He asked Tommy what he said.

"It's Christmas. The time of year, may it be always, for Jesus Christ."

The man groaned, "Oh, Jesus Christ!"

"Exactly. That's the idea."

The man looked at the little angel like he was a crazy person. "You thick or something?"

Tommy looked down at his body. "I have gotten larger very recently."

Mr. Mall Manager shook his head disgustedly. "Look, the two of you. The economy is in the crapper. We're having a horrible Christmas season. Sales are way down. So I can't get either of you a job. It's all about money. That's what Christmas is."

"No, it isn't. It's about peace and love and good will."

"Jesus Christ!"

Before Tommy could respond, the man said, "If you say 'exactly' one more time, I'll scream. Look," he added. "I gotta' go. I only have a few hours to sleep and I don't intend to waste them arguing with you two over a job that isn't going to happen."

Then he was out the door into the chill night air. He actually ran to his car, apparently to get away from his unwanted guests.

Tommy scratched his head. "Well, he certainly is not filled with the Christmas spirit!"

"Don't worry," Edward said. "I'm used to it. You have been kind to help," and he held out his hand. Tommy grasped it.

"We still can look elsewhere," Tommy said, but Edward shook his head.

"I will, but I don't want to bother you. Most people don't even treat me like a human being. You talked to me, shook my hand, went to bat for me. That is kindness enough. I cannot impose on your good nature any more. Merry Christmas, Tom."

"And to you, Edward."

Tommy made up his mind as Edward walked away that he would keep looking for a job for his new friend. He left the parking lot and walked back along the streets of Nanuet. Soon he saw lights and a sign. It was late, but at least one place was still open. "Skullduggery," the neon sign beckoned. "Bar and Grill." Tommy walked in. It was not like any restaurant his parents had ever taken him to. A disinterested bartender leaned over the bar watching an old *Magnum PI* show on TV.

Tommy asked the bartender if he went to Saint Anthony's.

"Nah. I work."

Tommy did not understand why the two were mutually exclusive, but the barkeep's tone held such finality that Tommy let it drop.

He next approached a solitary individual slumped on the bar next to a half-finished drink of some indeterminate amber color. Tommy asked if he went to the nearby church.

The man looked up. His breath stunk of what, Tommy did not know, and his eyes were bloodshot. "Yesh, I go sometimes," the man slurred.

Tommy said that was great. Did the man know Deacon John?

"Deacon?…Oh, John. Yeah. Great guy. If not fer him, we'd never go to the other ol' preis!"

Tommy then explained that he needed the man to come to Saint Anthony's right now to extol the deacon's virtues.

"I gosha' finish my drink, firs'. You know what, buddy?"

Tommy said he did not know.

"I love ya, buddy."

The man's head slumped to the counter. Tommy gently lifted him. His eyes flicked open. "I'll be shoor to see Deacon Shonn on Shunday," the man managed to utter. Then his head hit the counter again, not to be raised.

"Happens all the time, goddamn asshole," the bartender said. The barkeep was a burly fellow, so he had no trouble hoisting the patron, along with his coat, and depositing him on the pavement outside.

"He'll freeze out here!" Tommy protested.

"Nah. The cold'll wake him up eventually. He'll just piss all over himself and stumble home."

Tommy started to say that was outrageous. Seeing what was about to come, the barkeep headed it off at the pass. He grabbed a set of keys from the drunk's pocket, tossed them to Tommy and pointed at the fellow's car.

"He's in no shape to drive," Tommy said.

"Yuh think!" came the sarcastic reply. "If you want to be the Good Samaritan, you drive him home!" He pointed angrily. "Down the street, second left, last house on the right."

Tommy would have argued but, with a loud and rather emphatic curse, the barkeep stomped back into his lair. The unconscious man showed no signs of stirring, and Tommy feared he could die of exposure. It was below freezing at this hour of the night, and the wind had kicked up. Not gale force, but enough so that the cold seemed to cut right into your bones. With no shelter at hand, Tommy lifted the fellow. He was not all that heavy, especially given Tommy's adult size, and Tommy gently placed him in the passenger seat of the car. "He will be safe here," Tommy said to himself. Though the little angel had no way to know it, it had snowed lightly the day before his arrival. And while most of the light covering had melted that afternoon, in the freezing night air the wet surface of the road had become a sheet of black ice.

At least, Tommy reasoned, he had gotten the man off the frozen pavement. However, his view changed when a police cruiser stopped alongside him. The cop rolled down his window. "Sand and salt truck's coming by soon. You have to move that car, sir."

"Oh, but it is not my car. This gentleman here is, uh, sick and…"

"You have the keys?" the officer asked, seeing them dangling from Tommy's hands.

"Yes, sir."

"Move it! Now!"

"Could you do it?"

The cop got an angry look. "Listen, smartass! You move that car this second or I'll run you in!" The policeman stayed there glaring daggers at the little angel. Tommy reasoned it would be poor form to have to call the Almighty to bail him out of jail. Clearly the cop was not going away, so Tommy did what only seemed reasonable. He got in the car. He looked it over a minute.

"I'm only six!" he muttered. Of course he had never driven a car. However, he had watched his mom and dad drive countless times. It did not seem that hard. Besides, he was in a grown-up body, and an angel to boot now. What could go wrong?

It took three tries to thread the key into the ignition switch, and then Tommy held the ignition too long so the motor made a grinding sound. While the policeman had pulled out and turned off at the next block, Tommy guessed he might round the block and return, so he put the gear in drive and hit the pedal. Apparently he pressed too hard, for the car took off with a lurch. Tommy stomped on the brakes and the car stopped with a violent bucking motion. This lurching and bucking stage went on for about twenty feet until Tommy got the hang of it. The motion was so pronounced it seemed to shake the drinker from his torpor. "Thish boat's gonna' make me shick," he grumbled.

Tommy recalled the bartender's directions. Grasping the steering wheel with white-knuckle force, Tommy navigated the street and the second fast left without incident. He drove into the wrong lane, but at this hour there was no traffic and Tommy quickly compensated. His problem was not the turn. His problem was that the street his companion lived on was a hill. A steep hill, with a steep grade. To Tommy it looked like Mount Everest, and they were going downhill.

Now things happened quickly. Tommy mashed the accelerator, hitting a patch of ice. The car's tires, which had last seen tread in the Clinton administration, caused the car to fishtail and go into a skid.

Tommy cried out as the car hurtled downhill sideways on the slick ice. He frantically twirled the steering wheel this way and that, but had lost control.

All this motion and excitement finally woke the man completely. He stared bleakly at Tommy. "You're not mush of a driver," he said. Then his eyes grew wide and a measure of sobriety quickly returned, for through Tommy's side window, which was now the temporary front of the car, he saw at the bottom of the hill two huge machines spreading salt on the road—and heading directly for the fast-moving and out-of-control automobile.

Somewhere deep inside Tommy knew he was in no bodily danger, but if he was the cause of his passenger's death…well, if that was not reason for getting drummed out of the angel corps, nothing was. Tommy frantically turned the wheel.

"Turn in the direction of the skid," the man yelled, which to Tommy sounded like crazy talk.

Tommy did the only thing he could think of. He shut his eyes and cried out the only words that popped into his mind. "Holy Mary, Mother of God, pray for us sinners, now and at the hour of our death…!"

The car suddenly righted itself, hit a bump and hurtled into the air, passing directly over the salt trucks. It landed with a thud, skidded into the correct driveway and came to a halt an inch from the house.

"Amen!" Tommy concluded as he opened his eyes.

The passenger had never closed his eyes, however, and now he released his pent-up breath. "I need a drink!" he said in the quiet. Then he stumbled as he got out of the car, followed by Tommy, who helped him into his house.

Inside the man went to a cupboard and pulled out a bottle of gin. "Come on," he beckoned to Tommy.

"No," the angel replied. "That's what got you into trouble in the first place. By the power of God, you have just been given a wonderful gift. That," he indicated the bottle, "is something you do not need."

The man looked at Tommy for a long time. Then he stared at the bottle. Releasing another deep breath, and a lifetime of tension, he unscrewed the cap. Gave the bottle a last baleful look, then poured the contents down the drain in his kitchen sink. With Tommy's help, he went about emptying bottles and beer cans all over the house.

When Tommy turned to go the man asked who he was.

Tommy told him his name.

"I know that name," the man said. "Your family from Nyack?"

No, Tommy told him. It was a common name, but his parents still lived in Colonie. Near Albany.

"Well, no matter," the man, whose name was George, said as he poured himself a tall glass of Alka Seltzer. "You're my guardian angel."

"No," Tommy said, shaking his head. "Someone else has that job. He must have taken the night off, 'cause when I get back to heaven I'm going to give him hell."

That struck George as amusing. Even Tommy had to laugh. "Hey, Tommy," George said, "I have to go sleep this off. Then I'm going to do something I should have long ago. A good deed for the holiday." He held out a meaty paw. "Merry Christmas, Tommy."

Tommy took the proffered hand. "And a happy Christmas to you as well, George."

Tommy was about to enlist George's help in seeing to Deacon John, but just then George stumbled. He may have taken an important step toward recovering from his alcoholism, but it was evident he was ill tonight. Tommy told him to get to bed and, without complaint, George complied.

Tommy trudged back to the Skullduggery, where he was greeted by a frown from the bartender. There was only a couple left at the bar. A man and a woman, though Tommy did not realize this at first because the man was visiting the bathroom. So Tommy quite rationally assumed the woman was all alone. Aside from the bartender.

The woman had also been drinking, heavily. She wore a sequined dress as though she'd been at a formal event that evening. Tommy sat on a stool next to her and asked if she was a parishioner of Saint Anthony's. She seemed startled by the question.

"I guess," she wiped at a stray lock of hair. "But I haven't gone in years. I guess I've fallen away."

"Well, I'd like you to fall back," Tommy said, "at least for tonight."

The woman apparently misinterpreted what Tommy was asking. Her look turned…actually Tommy could not decipher

her look. But it was different. Similar to a look he sometimes saw Mom and Dad exchange when they shooed him off to bed.

The woman reached over and her nails dug playfully in the hair at the back of Tommy's neck. "Hey, you're cute," she said in a sultry voice.

All of a sudden Tommy felt a strong pull on his shoulder. He turned to see a tall man in a tuxedo jacket towering over him. Though tall, the man was not all that threatening on account of the fact he was unsteady on his feet. He was also sweating even though the bar was still chilly from when Tommy had entered.

"You tryin' to get together with my girl?" the fellow bellowed.

"Why, yes," Tommy said "I was hoping the two of us could go see Deacon John…"

"What! A three-way! With two guys! That is disgusting!"

"Oooh!" the woman cooed. "I think it's kind of interesting. Weird, but interesting."

The man shot her a look. "Keep out of this, Liz."

Tommy was not sure why the man was so angry. Perhaps because he had been excluded from the conversation, though even at that his reaction seemed over the top. So Tommy politely invited the gentlemen to join them.

"Listen, buddy!" the man yelled. "You must be one sick bastard! You want me to make hamburger meat out of you?"

Thinking of his non-corporeal nature, Tommy responded, "I don't think you can do that."

Unfortunately everything Tommy said to try to defuse the situation only made the man angrier. This being no exception. The man lifted Tommy off his stool and pushed him toward the door. "Do you want to see what I can do?"

Just then Tommy noticed a flower in the man's lapel, which made Tommy think he might be some sort of magician. "I *would* like to see what you can do, especially if it involves neat tricks!" Tommy said.

"Tricks!" the man roared. "You accusin' Liz of turning tricks?"

To Tommy's innocent mind it had an entirely different connotation. "Is she your assistant?" Tommy asked in an excited voice. "I bet you two are great at tricks!"

The man slammed his fist on the bar, then hauled off and unleashed a mighty roundhouse right.

"Jesus, Mary and Joseph!" Tommy thought as he closed his eyes.

The only question was who was more surprised, Tommy or his attacker. Tommy felt nothing when the fist passed through his body. It was as if he were made of air. The force of the blow and the lack of impact caused the man, already inebriated, to spin around, lose his balance and collapse onto a nearby chair, which promptly smashed to pieces.

"That's going onto your tab!" the bartender called out, otherwise staying uninvolved.

Tommy helped the man in the tuxedo to his feet. "Wha' happened?" the man said as he slowly regained his footing, intending to repay Tommy's kindness with another blow. "I'll kill you, bud!"

"I'll tell you what happened, Fred," the woman cried out. "Your insane jealousy has gotten the best of you. This nice man," she indicated Tommy, "easily evaded you and helped you up, and still you are breathing fire. Well, I've had enough of it! You change your behavior this minute, or I am leaving you—forever!"

The man looked down sheepishly. Then he glanced up at Tommy. "You weren't hitting on my girl?"

Tommy smiled. "I would never hit a girl!"

Now Liz seemed annoyed. "What? I'm not good enough for you?" she demanded, glaring at Tommy.

"You dissing my girl?" Fred said as menace crept back into his features.

Tommy held his palms up. "Ma'am. You are a very pretty lady, but please believe I had no intention of inappropriate behavior. You deserve better than that."

"You see, Fred?" she said. "He is a gentleman. Now what do you say?"

Fred looked down again, then held out his hand. "I'm sorry," he said in a very low voice.

"Louder!" Liz prodded.

"Sorry," and he thrust his hand forward.

It occurred to Tommy that there was a lot about adult behavior he didn't understand. He shook Fred's hand warmly.

"Will you be my witness?" Liz asked Tommy.

The angel was not sure what was coming, but he agreed. "I am a witness to the Lord, after all."

Liz's smile lit up the room. "Hey, I like that. What is your name?"

Tommy told her and Fred his name.

"You're new here?" she asked.

"You might say that," Tommy replied. "My parents still live in Colonie."

Liz asked if he would be visiting them.

Tommy grimaced and said he could not. Business obligations.

Turning to her boyfriend, Liz said, "What about it, Fred? Will you find it in your heart to be more of a—pacifist—like Tommy here? As he is the Lord's witness?"

"I will...if..."

"If what?"

"If you agree to marry me. I love you, Liz, and I will change for you. I just can't stand the thought of losing you."

Liz flung herself into Fred's arms, and Tommy sensed it was time for him to leave. He still had to find someone to help

Deacon John. As they kissed deeply (which made Tommy go "yuck!" to himself), the angel left the bar.

Tommy had not walked far when a woman in a doorway called out to him. "Hey, handsome, you like to have a good time?"

"Certainly," Tommy answered as he looked the woman over. He could not help it, for she wore an excessive amount of makeup. Though what struck him more was her dress. Or rather, the lack thereof. It was a frigid night and she wore practically nothing. Her top was cut so low, Tommy could see a generous helping of her breasts, which were rather large. That was not all he saw, for in the cold the outline of her nipples extended way out through the flimsy top. Her skirt covered as little of her bottom as the shirt did of her top. A lot of leg showed.

Tommy immediately took off his coat and draped it around her. "You must be freezing!" he said.

"A gentleman," she cooed. "Thank you. I don't usually get such a kind reaction. But I don't mind the cold. After all, I have to show off my wares."

Tommy looked at her, perplexed.

"You know," she said. "To get guys interested."

"Gosh," Tommy mused, "adults are so strange."

The woman, who on further observation had to be no more than twenty-five, asked Tommy if he wanted to get out of the cold. The building behind them was where she lived.

Tommy knew he had to find help for Deacon John but also now felt obligated to get this poor girl into warmth lest she catch her death of cold. He followed her into her apartment building while she held his coat close around her.

Inside her apartment, the woman poured two cups of coffee. "We'll warm up first, then get down to business." She had taken Tommy's coat off and crossed her legs, allowing her skirt to rise up even higher. It looked like she had no underwear on,

Tommy's startled eyes saw. The woman appeared pleased by his look. She said as much. "You like what you see?"

"I guess," he answered politely.

She gave him that sultry look he had seen from Liz in the bar earlier in the evening, and then she shook out her hair. "Hold the cup with both hands," she insisted.

Tommy obliged but asked why.

"So your hands will not be like ice when we start."

"Start what?"

Another coy smile. "A little petting. Then some oral stimulation. And then, if you are a good boy, no, make that if you are a bad boy," she slapped his thigh, "a little more." She paused before adding, "I would like a hundred twenty-five dollars."

How sad, Tommy thought. Another unemployed person.

"I do not have any money," he said, "but…"

She cut him off. "Then what the hell are you doing here?"

"You invited me in. And I am not here in the name of hell but in the name of heaven."

It was her turn to look puzzled. "You want me to dress up like a nun?"

Tommy shrugged. "If you wish."

"We're not doing anything without money," she snarled. "Just my luck. The only guy I attract tonight and it turns out he has no money."

"Money isn't everything," Tommy said.

"Hah! What's more important than money?"

"Love."

"You believe in all that mush?"

"What is your name?"

"Dana."

"Dana." Tommy looked at her so searchingly, Dana squirmed in her seat. "Dana," Tommy repeated, "how could you not feel love? How about from your mother?"

Dana bit her lip. "She died when I was…"

"Six," Tommy finished the thought.

She looked up in surprise. "How did you know?"

"A little angel told me," he responded truthfully.

"Don't you mean a little birdie?"

"No, I mean a little angel."

Dana got a far-off look. "I miss my mother so much. I remember when I was little, how Mama would kiss my knee when I fell and caress my forehead when I was sick, and she always sang to me. She loved to sing." Her eyes misted. "Yes, I did feel loved then, but that was so long ago."

"She's still there for you, Dana."

"But how?"

Tommy pointed upward. "In heaven."

"It's been so long, sometimes I can hardly remember what she looked like. Isn't that sad? There was a fire shortly after Mama died and I lost all my pictures of her. God, how I wish I could believe she was in heaven."

"You can. When your Mama passed away, don't you remember anything strange happening?"

She thought a second. "How do you know this stuff? Yes. Yes! I had forgotten, but you're right! For about a week after I got home from school the phone rang. There was never anyone on the line but I know it was her. You see, when she was alive she always called from work at that same time, to make sure I had gotten home from school all right."

"That was a sign," Tommy told her.

"How could it be?"

"I have heard that the recently departed are allowed one way to contact their loved ones to let them know they are safe."

"Maybe." She appeared unconvinced but beginning to wonder. "But it was so long ago. And I have not felt anything remotely resembling love since she left me."

Tommy told her love was something you had to search for. Put yourself in the right situations. "You hide in the doorway in the dark, you're going to meet a different type of person than if you go to church or help out in hospitals," he said.

Dana sniffed. "Guys just want one thing, and it isn't love. Especially with someone like me. I mean, I know I'm not all that pretty, but I do have a great body."

"Nonsense. You are very pretty, under all that makeup. Besides, it isn't just about looks."

"You think I'm pretty?"

"Of course. More importantly, I perceive that you have a good heart."

"No one's ever said that to me."

"No one said the world was round until Columbus. That did not make the place flat, however. Trust me. You have such goodness within you, a lot of capacity to love—and be loved. Isn't that what your mother would say?"

Dana put her face in her hands and cried. "She would be ashamed of me!"

Tommy told her she was wrong. "She is your mother. She loves you and would want you to get back on the path of love."

Dana touched Tommy's face. Carefully. "Would you... would you be interested in someone like me?"

"I would, but it is not possible. You see, I am...I am... different."

"Are you gay?"

"I am happy a lot."

Dana giggled. "No. What I mean is, do you dig guys?"

Tommy blushed. "No, not in that sense. I am dedicated to the Lord. I can't explain it any better than that."

"You mean like a priest?"

"Something like that."

Dana confided that she had a peaceful feeling being around Tommy.

"Talking helps," he said.

"Maybe. But there is something different about you. Am I right?"

Tommy did not know what to say without revealing his true identity. He did not have to say anything, however, because Dana filled in the silence. "You have been very kind, but I just don't know."

Tommy nodded. "Would you let me help you? To believe once again, I mean. Here, take this. It's a small present for you. Merry Christmas, Dana." He leaned over and kissed her lightly on the cheek. From out of nowhere Tommy handed her a small prettily wrapped package.

It had been years since Dana had received a gift with no strings attached. With a resplendent grin, she carefully removed the wrapping, as if she wanted to savor and hold on to the moment. "Oh, my God!" she cried out when it was opened, genuine tears coursing down her cheeks as she stared at the gift. What Dana was looking at was a photograph—of her mother!

When she had regained a semblance of control she wiped at her eyes and nose. Looking up she started to ask, "How did you ever...?" But Dana stopped abruptly, because no one was there. She turned her head quickly, but there was no one in her tiny apartment. Even Tommy's coat had disappeared. Dana ran to the door and threw it open. Yet in every direction she looked...there was absolutely no one to be seen. There was no way Tommy could have moved that fast.

Tears again came and Dana, clutching the sacred photo to her chest, looked up to the sky. "Oh, my God!" she again cried out. "Mama! Oh, Mama! Thank you!" Then her tears mingled with laughter. After many moments had passed, Dana went inside and to the bathroom, where she wiped off every last trace of makeup. Then she looked at her wall calendar. "It's Christmas Eve," she whispered, somewhat in wonder. Dana picked through her clothes, trying to locate the most conservative outfit she owned, then went to her cheap computer to look up something on the Internet. Gazing fondly at the picture of her mother, which she realized she'd been caressing, she promised her mother that just as they had done when she was little, she would attend Christmas services. Online, she looked up the information on the Saint Anthony's website.

.   .   .

In another part of town, Tommy looked at a clock. It was almost four forty-five. Not much time left and he had yet to locate a soul to help him. Dana might have been a possibility, but she was so emotionally fragile at this moment, Tommy did not want to burden her with Deacon John's woes. He also did not see how he could enlist Dana's aid now after delivering her gift without revealing his angelic nature. With no idea how to proceed, Tommy returned to the church.

He frowned to see that the door was locked. Tommy passed through the solid oak anyway as only angels can, but inside it was empty as could be. It was five o'clock in the morning. Deacon John had probably left earlier to catch his bus. Tommy wanted to kick himself. Why had he left the deacon alone to succumb to the voices?

The slightest tinge of despair crept into Tommy's head. What if God was right? Forget about finding five people of good will. Tommy had not been able to find a single one. He was truly at a loss. Looking up at the main altar, he cried out, "What do I do now?"

Suddenly Tommy felt a presence next to him in the pew. "Oh, thank God you're here, Jesse!" A pause and Tommy added, "You are here, aren't you?" He said this because Jesse's image was flickering, as if he were an apparition.

"Like all guardian angels, I am always around for you. But I am not there in bodily form. I am still in the other realm."

Tommy said, "But I am fully here."

"That's because you were sent on a mission to Earth. I was not."

"Oh. Did you ever have a mission here?"

"Three times, actually. Most of us do. It was very long ago, however."

"How did it go?"

"Tommy, it's a long story and I don't have the time right now. There is another matter upstairs that I have to attend to."

"Before you go, can you help me?"

"That is why I am here. Well, partially here. Your problem is that you are thinking too much. You are trying to solve it like a human. What you need is to approach it as an angel would."

"What does that mean exactly? How do I think like an angel?"

"For starters, don't over-think it. Follow your heart."

"What kind of advice is that?"

Jesse's image was fading.

"No! Don't leave yet, Jesse! I need real guidance, not unfathomable clues. What should I do?"

There was no response and Tommy let his arm fall to the pew dejectedly. "Follow my heart," he muttered. "Fifteen billion years since Creation and that's the best they can come up with?" He sat in the quiet, the only noises the occasional hiss from the heater and the crackle of the votive candles.

"If I were to follow my heart, what would I do?" Then Tommy smacked his head. "Stop thinking," he whispered in the quiet. He just sat there in the silence, hoping inspiration would fill the void. Tommy turned to look at the small wall clock in the rear of the church and saw he only had about forty minutes before the deacon's bus would depart. No doubt John was at the terminal now. "I ought to go visit him," Tommy said quietly, rising to leave the church yet again.

At this early hour the world was just waking up, so there was not a lot of human traffic yet. That made it easier for Tommy to use his angel sense to pop in and out of places unnoticed. Which is how he instantaneously arrived at the bus station, relieved that for once his sense of direction was spot on. Aside from the sleepy-looking ticket taker behind a barred window, only a half dozen passengers waited on benches in the waiting area. One was napping and two were in deep contemplation over their Starbucks. Three others were absorbed in reading; two had the newspaper and one was engrossed in a paperback. In the far corner of the passenger wait area, sitting off by himself, was Deacon John. Tommy had popped in unnoticed and he quietly walked over to John, sat on the bench next to him and bid him hello.

"Oh!" John said, a little startled. "I guess I was daydreaming. I didn't expect to ever see you again."

"I said I would be back," Tommy replied pleasantly.

"People say a lot of things to be polite but never really mean them." The deacon thought a moment, then said, "I guess you are not most people."

"If you only knew!" The words popped out of Tommy's mouth before he realized what he was saying. Fortunately John did not discern anything untoward in Tommy's remark. Before the deacon had a chance to reflect on what Tommy had said, the angel quickly added, "I had to come back. I just could not let you leave without seeing you one more time."

"Why? You don't really know me. We only just met."

"Haven't you ever bonded right away with someone at first sight? Didn't you say that about when you met your wife? I know a lot more about you than you think."

"Why bother?" John asked. "Why is this so important to you?"

"Because your leaving is a huge mistake. I'm just trying to right a wrong—before it happens."

"No offense, but what do you know?"

"I know that your doubts are misplaced. There is a God. And a heaven. And your daughter—and your wife—are very happy there looking over you."

John looked at Tommy sadly. "God, how I wish I could believe once again that were true."

And in that instant it came to Tommy. He could not stand by and let this good man hurt so much. "Close your eyes for a moment, John." There was something in Tommy's tone that was so compelling, John could not refuse. He closed his eyes. Tommy placed his hands over John's head. And the doubting deacon saw.

It was a glorious image. Someplace John could not make out, but he could tell it was peaceful and serene and beautiful. In the center of it…was Clare! She looked up, gazing directly into John's eyes. "Oh Daddy! I love you so much! I want you to know that I'm all right. Also that I am so proud, so very, very proud of you. What you did for that couple the night I died is something I will carry with me forever. It was even better than if you could have been with me in my last minutes."

John's voice broke and tears were running down his cheeks. "I didn't let you down?"

"Of course not. You raised me up. Just as you have always done all through my life. Listen, Daddy. We do not have much time, but there is someone else I want you to see." In that instant, Holly appeared beside their daughter.

"Holly!" John called. "I've missed you so much!"

Holly smiled at her husband. "We will be together soon. Before you know it. You did a wonderful job with her, John. Thank you. For that and for all the love I still feel for you. We will be waiting for you."

"This seems so real."

"It is. Love is our reality," Holly told him.

Clare spoke again. "We have to go, Daddy. The angel is only allowed to share the vision with you for a short time." Then Clare shared a favorite saying of Tommy's. "Daddy, Mommy and I want you to always remember: Those who believe in Jesus never see each other for the last time."

John's tears were replaced by a wide smile and a placid expression. When he opened his eyes to thank Tommy...there was no one there! An elderly woman stepped in front of John to the counter, asking for a ticket to Florida.

Deacon John jumped up and said, "That will not be necessary. Here, take my ticket. I won't be needing it. I have to get back to the church."

When John opened the terminal door, the wind kicked up and a voice started to say something. John whispered, "Begone, Satan! The Lord your God shall you worship, and Him only shall you serve."

There was a last painful howl and the wind was gone. As was the voice. As was Deacon John, who would serve the parish many a long year, ever grateful for his Christmas dream.

✦ Three ✦

Tommy had two powerful emotions one right after the other. The first was an overwhelming sense of joy, followed by an almost equally powerful dread. The reason for the first was the angel's success with Deacon John. The tale of Michael and the archangels defeating Satan through love suddenly began to take on tangible meaning.

The angel was in a different part of town now. He still did not trust his sense of direction to take lengthy angelic leaps, so he merely transported himself a few blocks away. At that, he was several streets away from the spot he had intended. So for now it would be short hops until he got the hang of it.

The reason for his dread was the realization that he had inadvertently stumbled into a pit. "I came here to do two easy tasks. Assure my parents, and find five men or women of good will to show God." Having gotten sidetracked with Deacon John, as well as with Edward, George, Fred, Liz and Dana, Tommy had lost valuable time. It was now Christmas Eve morning. He had less than a day remaining on Earth. Worse, his tasks were multiplying. He had taken on a third, the deacon, and now a fourth beckoned, that of trying to assist Edward and his family this Christmas season. As if doubling his task list in half the time was not problem enough (Tommy had never taken algebra, but he supposed there was a mathematical equation indicating how far he had regressed), Tommy had forfeited a valuable tool. By following his heart and sharing the supernatural vision with Deacon John, he had surrendered his best asset to ease his parents' anguish. The one vision he was allowed to share had been used up, and Tommy certainly knew he could not request another. He sat on a bench by a park, abandoned in the cold. He looked nostalgically at the monkey bars. How he'd loved to climb them in the old, uncomplicated days. Was it really only a few months ago? It seemed like a lifetime, which in a sense it was.

Tommy was a very organized fellow, so he decided he would take care of Edward and his destitute family first. Then his parents, and then he would do the bidding of the Almighty. He did not have a clue as to how he would soothe his parents without the ability to share a vision or to otherwise reveal himself. Oh, well, he would make it up as he went along. "God provides," he thought, "just like Mom used to say."

While still staring at the jungle gym, Tommy felt a nudge. It was a policeman with his billy club. "No loitering!" he snapped.

Tommy looked about. "I didn't drop any trash."

The cop made a face. "I didn't say littering, you fool. I said *loitering*. You are not allowed to sit here."

"But it is a bench. That seems like a stupid rule," Tommy commented.

"I'm not gonna' debate it with you. It's so children can't be preyed upon."

The little angel did not follow. He explained to the officer that he was just watching the monkey bars, hoping children would come there to play.

"Oh, you like little children?"

"Yes, I do very much. I would happily play with them now if they were out."

The cop got a disgusted look and said, "Move it along, creep! Before I run you in!"

Tommy obliged, wondering why all the police he met were so surly. Come to think of it, it was not just the police. Down here people from all walks of life seemed to be irritable. Finding those five people seemed more and more like a mountainous challenge.

Since a journey of a thousand miles begins with a single step, Tommy took his first one in the opposite direction of the policeman. Some small shops were opening up now, so Tommy made his way for them. First was a Starbucks. Tommy waited his turn in line. Once at the head he asked for a job for his friend Edward. The harried sales girl called the manager over. He told Tommy he wasn't hiring on account of the recession. "We're struggling," the man said. "Would you like to order anything?"

"How can you be struggling?" Tommy asked. "There's a Starbucks every fifty feet."

"That's corporate," the manager said. "I'm just one unlucky franchisee."

Tommy did not know what a franchisee was. He assumed it was a sect he had not heard of. Like the Baptists or something.

Someone in the back of the growing line called out, "Hey, is that guy ordering or making a speech?"

Tommy turned and explained, "I am trying to help my fellow man."

"Well, help him someplace else. We want our coffee!"

At least three voices were raised in agreement, one of which let Tommy know in expletive force what its owner thought of him. Tommy's faith in humanity was further shaken. "Maybe God ought to just send another flood and be done with it!" he murmured.

"Darn," the woman immediately behind him said, apparently having overheard him. "And I didn't bring my umbrella today!"

The manager waved a barista over to take orders and led Tommy to the side, off the customer line. He said it was their busiest time of year, so he could not stand there and yak all day. "I don't have forever."

"Actually, you do," Tommy said.

The manager calmly but firmly told Tommy that although he was short-handed and overworked, he could not afford to hire anyone, even on a temporary basis.

"I just want to do something for his family this Christmas."

In his best Marie Antoinette "let them eat cake" voice, the manager said, "Get them a present." That actually struck Tommy as a great idea. If he could not get Edward a job, perhaps he could find some presents to brighten the sad family's day. Tommy said as much to the manager and asked what he could contribute to the cause. The man grunted and walked back toward the cash register. Tommy's heart soared. A healthy financial donation would be most welcome. Instead, the man grabbed a mug with the corporate logo from a rack near the register. He returned and thrust it at Tommy. "Here!" he said, and he was off.

Back on the sidewalk one of a group of children walking by ran up to Tommy. At first blush the child looked familiar. Tommy thought it might be a playmate of his. However it could only be a resemblance, since Tommy had lived over a hundred miles from here. So Tommy was stunned when the kid grabbed the mug, hurled it to the ground, smashing it to pieces, and ran away, yelling, "Merry Christmas, asshole!" to the shouts of accompanying laughter from his friends.

Tommy looked after the boy sadly. "If even the children have gone bad, it's worse than I feared." He thought of Mom and Dad and the people in his tiny circle of the living in his old hometown. "No," Tommy said out loud. "People are not mean everywhere. My luck is bound to turn."

He tried to find Edward a job at a fish store, flower shop and convenience mart in that order with as little success as at the coffee shop. He did get twenty-five dollars, courtesy of the seafood market, and a flower from the florist. The angel was passing a bus stop. The small line waiting for the express bus to mid-town was huddled together against the chill. Two people wiped at their runny noses. One woman, probably thirtyish, had a particularly nasty look. "She must also have had a rough night," Tommy thought as he approached and gave her the flower. "For you, Miss. Merry Christmas!" he said in a chipper tone.

The woman's eyes narrowed. "You...are...not...getting...in...my...pants," she hissed and walked to the trash can, where she crumpled and tossed the flower.

Tommy did not linger to ask why she thought he would want her pants. He wondered if he had been sent to a bizarro world by mistake.

"I only meant it as a sincere gesture," he told her.

"F--- you!" she got close to his face, using the full emphasis of the expletive.

Tommy walked off as the bus came just then. He had not traveled far when he heard a child crying. A little girl had taken a spill over a patch of ice. Tommy ran and helped her to her feet. Hugging the weeping child, he asked where it hurt. Soundlessly, but for the sniffles, she pointed to her knee. Sure enough the fabric on her pants was torn and when Tommy gently rolled up her cuff he saw that she had skinned her knee. Nothing serious, but Tommy had had many a similar tumble in his brief six years on Earth.

Remembering what his mother had done countless times, Tommy put his finger to his lips, kissed it and held it lightly to the cut. He knew there was no medicinal value but for the fact of a mother's love, or in this case a helper's love. The girl stopped crying instantly and Tommy indicated the spot where she fell. "Were you trying to break the sidewalk? There's a crack there."

The little girl giggled and Tommy removed his finger from the cut. To his amazement, the scrape had completely healed.

Frowning, Tommy rolled the pants back down and repeated the gesture over the tear in the girl's pants. It, too, healed itself. The girl giggled once more and asked if Tommy was a "'gician." It was in that instant that Tommy realized his angel powers were growing. Jesse had told him that would be the case, but to actually experience it in real time was an amazing thing to behold. Tommy's angel powers were not enough to get him away from what happened next, however.

There was a loud shriek. "Get away from her!" A woman was hurtling down the street toward Tommy, screaming, "Sara! Sara! Are you all right?"

When she got there, panting, she practically tore Sara from Tommy's arms and again growled at him. "Don't you ever touch my child! I ought to call the police!" Turning to the girl she said, "Why did you run off like that? I was buying a newspaper and the next thing I knew, you were gone! I was frantic with worry!"

"I wanted to play on the ice, but I fell. This man was very nice," Sara explained. "He made my knee and my pants all better. I think he's a 'gician."

Mother turned back to Tommy. He expected an apology from her now that Sara had straightened things out. Then Tommy intended to enlist the mother's help in his quest. She was dressed in a business suit under her winter coat, so she must have some pull in the world of commerce. Perhaps she could help Edward and his family. What Tommy received was not even remotely close to an apology. With a stern look the woman barked, "All the same, a word of advice. Keep your hands off my child and any child for that matter. We can't be too careful with all the cases of child abuse around."

Then she picked up Sara and stomped off. "I wonder if she works at Scrooge and Marley," Tommy said to himself. Then he wondered if Jesus were alive today and said, "Suffer the little children and forbid them not to come unto Me," would He be prosecuted for his efforts?

At the corner a Salvation Army volunteer had just set up his pot and was starting to ring a bell.

Tommy stopped, explained about Edward's plight and asked if he could take money out of the pot for the poor family.

The volunteer looked at Tommy like the angel had three heads. "You touch that pot and I'll yell for the police!" Since Tommy's two encounters with the law enforcement establishment had been less than pleasant, he opted to forego the pleasure this time around and moved on. The man called after him, "You should be ashamed of yourself! Trying to take money donated for the poor and needy!"

"Why should I be ashamed of helping the poor and needy?" was Tommy's thought. He looked skyward. "Lord, I know it looks bad, but I still don't think this is as godless a people as they seem. Strange, yes, but not bad. Maybe they have just lost their way."

A little further on Tommy saw a young man playing a violin on the street corner. The musician had long hair. He was playing Christmas carols mostly, but old ones, the ones you only heard nowadays on classical music stations. Songs like *Il Est Ne Le Divine Enfant* and *Here We Go A Wassailing*. Tommy smiled as he stopped to enjoy the heavenly music. That was an apt description, for the young man was genuinely talented. He was as good as one of the saintly violinists Tommy had heard rehearsing in heaven the other day. That violinist had been limbering up for a performance of a new symphony by Beethoven. Beethoven's one hundred forty-sixth, actually. "If you thought his first nine were good, you haven't heard anything yet," Jesse had confided.

Anyway, there was a box next to the violinist. He had attracted some stray change. One passerby, however, did not slow his stride or deposit a coin as he muttered, "Damn long-hair freak."

Tommy wanted to point out that Jesus had long hair also, but he perceived all it would merit was an angry display of the gentleman's middle finger. When the violinist finished *Il Est Ne*, which had been Tommy's favorite (his mother used to sing it a lot, in French) the angel applauded heartily. The violinist bowed and thanked him. "You're out of work, too?" the musician asked.

Tommy allowed as he had no job. "But I see you're doing okay," he added, nodding toward the box. While it was nowhere near full, it contained many more coins than Edward had been able to net in his cap outside the mall yesterday evening.

The musician said it was enough to help him scrape by. That, and he earned a few bucks giving lessons. "You know what really gets me through the day?" he asked Tommy. "Every so often someone stops to enjoy my playing and gets so caught up in the music they miss their bus. I get great pleasure out of that. More than the money."

Tommy was puzzled. "You like people to be late for work?" He wondered if this was some sort of misery-loves-company thing.

"No." The violinist smiled, introducing himself as Todd. "What I meant is that if I am good enough that my music diverts them from what they were doing, well, it gives me a real sense of accomplishment. It's about the only thing that helps me persevere."

"How so?" Tommy asked.

"Do you know what it's like trying to crack into this field? It's darn near impossible. I haven't been able to get anyone in the business to recognize my talent. I have to tell you, it gets me real down sometimes."

Todd said it was time for him to get back to his music. He asked if Tommy had any requests and was surprised when Tommy asked if he knew *In Dulci Jubilo*. Todd managed a wide grin and again bowed. "You are a discerning music aficionado," he said. "Most people ask for *Jingle Bells*, or *Deck the Halls*, or even something vulgar like *Grandma Got Run Over By a Reindeer."* He shook his head, then launched into a spirited rendition of the old-time favorite.

By the time Todd finished, seven other listeners had congregated. They all joined Tommy in enthusiastic applause. A few coins and dollar bills found their way into the collection box. Tommy approached his musician friend one last time. "Here," he whispered confidentially. "I don't want to leave this to the vagaries of the box. It is all I have." The angel thrust the twenty-five dollars he had into Todd's palm.

Then Tommy asked why, if Todd wanted to get noticed, he didn't seek out more promising venues where he might get discovered, like church choirs and such.

"I've tried," Todd said glumly. "They were all filled up, or didn't know what use to make of a violinist. Most of the local choirs are choral only, with just an organist for accompaniment."

The angel asked if Todd knew where Saint Anthony's was. "Go there and ask for Deacon John. Tell him Tommy sent you. I am sure he will get you into tonight's midnight Mass. But remember to ask for Deacon John only. If you see an old priest, avoid him like the plague."

The import of what Tommy had just offered hit Todd, while the violinist unrumpled the dollars in his palm. He had never been given so much for street entertainment. His eyes bugged out and he thanked Tommy profusely.

Tommy made a show of checking his watch, which of course he did not have. "Ohmygosh! I'm late!"

As the little angel scurried off, Todd called after him with a huge grin, "You've made me triply happy! What can I do to repay the kindness?"

Todd's benefactor was a distance away by now as he called over his shoulder. Todd couldn't be sure but it sounded like Tommy said, "Go and sin no more."

Chuckling, Todd said, "This just might be the best Christmas ever!" He pocketed his earnings, packed up and headed off in search of this Deacon John.

Tommy, meanwhile, still had that uneasy feeling. "I am doing well," he thought, "but I am no closer to completing my assigned tasks." His long strides had taken him away from the tiny town's business district to a residential area. Cheered by his encounter with the gifted musical virtuoso, Tommy felt optimistic. Maybe in this neighborhood he would experience a change of luck.

Not a third of the way down the street the angel heard a voice from on high call out, "Yoo hoo! Yoo hoo!" He looked up to the heavens but could not see anyone. Nor did he sense Jesse, Gabriel or anyone from the other world. "Strange," he muttered as he took another step—and heard it again. Looking about some more, Tommy now saw an odd sight: an old woman in a doorway waving what appeared to be a flag in his direction.

"You!" the woman called out again.

Tommy looked behind him. And to the left and right. He pointed to himself questioningly. The old woman nodded excitedly. So Tommy walked up her drive.

"Young man, could you do me a favor? My arthritis is acting up something awful and I cannot manage to get down these stairs. Could you get the mail for me?"

Such a simple request. The mailbox was on the street. Tommy did not mind. He opened the tiny box and removed a small packet of letters, bringing them to the woman without looking at the post.

When he handed them to her she proclaimed, "Oh, thank you so much. You were the third person I had to ask. I guess you're my Good Samaritan." She laughed.

Tommy frowned. "You mean two others refused to help you?"

"I guess they were busy." She did not look happy as she said it and as she tore through the mail. "Oh, dear," she said.

Tommy asked if something was wrong.

"My daughter was going to send me bus fare so I could visit her and her family for Christmas. I was hoping it would arrive in time. But…well, you know how the mail is this time of year."

"What will you do?"

She gave a brave smile. "Oh, it's all right. I will just stay here for the holiday. Can't really maneuver with these joints of mine anyway. I suppose my daughter's gift will come the day after Christmas and I will at least get to spend New Year's with them."

"You have a good attitude about your misfortune."

She gave an impish grin. "At my age if I am on this side of the ground when I wake up, it's a good day. What's not to have a fine attitude about?"

Tommy wished her luck and turned to go.

"Excuse me. My name is Marsha. Marsha Kimball." She held out a bony and gnarled hand which Tommy took, telling her his name in return.

Marsha asked if he would like hot cocoa.

Tommy said he would love to but he had some business to attend to.

"I understand, dear. I hope you did not think me forward. It's just that I do not get any visitors."

She slowly turned to go and started to shut the door.

Tommy had an immediate change of heart. "Uh, Ma'am?" he said.

She turned back. "Please. It's Marsha."

"Marsha, Ma'am," Tommy found it hard to address his elders by their first names. "I spoke hastily. I know as soon as you close that door I will have a hankering for a cup of hot chocolate."

The resulting smile could have lit up the nearest star system and seemed to take years off her face as Marsha flung the door wide open.

Inside it was cozy and warm and had a smell reminiscent of Tommy's grandmother's house. He wondered if all grandparent homes contained this unique but welcoming smell.

In the center of the small living room was a Christmas tree with just a few ornaments and no lights. The few balls on it were pretty, however, and personalized. Tommy complimented Marsha on her tree.

She laughed. "Oh, it's just a Charlie Brown sort of tree, I know. But at my age it is all I can cope with."

When Tommy asked about the origin of the ornaments she proudly told him she had made them years ago. "I used to be very good at crafts."

"Wow! I can see that." There were a few ornaments with pictures of children. These ones she had made of her daughter at various stages of youth. Tommy gently fingered a gleaming white crocheted angel. It made him smile. Looking at the old lady questioningly, he saw her nod. "Yes, I made that too. Back when these fingers worked properly."

Something else caught Tommy's eye. On a small demilune against the wall was the most exquisite crèche scene he had ever witnessed. The figures appeared to be made of marble and the expressions on the faces were so lifelike. The angel asked Marsha about it.

"Oh," she blushed as she clutched at her neckline. "I made that as well. Years ago, when these old fingers were much more nimble." It turned out the figures were ceramic. Tommy asked if she used a mold. "Of course. Not store bought, mind you. I designed the molds myself."

Tommy's eyes widened. "*You* drew up your own molds? That's incredible! These are so real-looking!"

The old lady appeared deeply touched by the fact that any-one noticed she once had something meaningful to contribute, and that her art still carried a visceral wallop. She led Tommy off to the pint-size kitchen. He had to take a last lingering glance at the nativity set. "However did you capture Mary's likeness? It looks just like her!"

Marsha said she just saw it in her mind. "Of course we won't know how accurately I did until the time comes when we see the Blessed Mother in the hereafter."

Tommy shook his head and, using his new power, whistled softly. "You nailed it," he exclaimed in a whisper.

Over cocoa Marsha dominated the conversation. Several times she apologized for prattling on so, but Tommy waved her off each time. He sensed she needed this. Besides, to share a moment of attention with another person was so small an effort on his part.

At one point Marsha shared the tidbit that her condition did not hamper her walking. Just going up and down stairs. That was why she was a prisoner in the house whenever the condition acted up. The front stoop was too daunting.

"What if you had a ramp installed?" Tommy asked.

"That would work, but I do not have the funds to pay for such an extravagance. I had it priced out once. Do you know what it would cost?"

Tommy shook his head. She leaned over and whispered in his ear. Even Tommy was shocked by the amount.

"It's too bad," Marsha sighed. "When Herb was alive, he was my husband, you know, he could have whipped it up in no time flat. He was very good with his hands. Why, I still have a pile of lumber in the back. He was going to build a gazebo so I could sit in the summer and enjoy the flowers. It was going to be our fiftieth anniversary gift." She made another sigh. "The problem was he died months after we had our forty-ninth."

She looked up and swatted at an imaginary impediment. "Oh, go shoo! Let's not talk about sad things. I had forty-nine wonderful years with Herb and have lived just fine without a gazebo. Or a ramp, for that matter. I get by."

A sip of hot chocolate and Marsha looked up at Tommy. "You know, you're a good listener. Just being in your presence makes me feel better."

Tommy said he was glad for that.

She chuckled. "You remind me a lot of Herb. He was a dear, dear man and also a wonderful listener. He used to say he loved the sound of my voice, but I never could tell if he meant it or just said it to be polite. But I loved it all the same."

Tommy got a funny look just for a second. He cocked his head to the side and said, "Oh, he meant it, all right. Herb did indeed thrill to the sound of your voice. He still does."

She waved Tommy off. "Oh, go on. You are too kind to say so."

Tommy just smiled at his little secret.

The old woman was about to say something when the unmistakable sound of a telephone ringing could be heard. It was most definitely not Marsha's, and Tommy had no phone. They do not use cell phones in heaven and other than the new clothes and coat to fit his newly adult frame, the archangels sent him with no extraneous equipment. Tommy knew that, but to his surprise and initial embarrassment, he realized the noise was coming from him!

"Uh, excuse me. I have to take this."

Marsha nodded indulgently and said, "By all means."

Tommy was in a mild panic because he did not know what he was taking exactly, or how. With no better idea, he turned from Marsha and reached into his coat pocket as if retrieving a cell phone. He then spoke into his semi-closed palm. To his considerable surprise the ringing stopped and there was a person on the other end. "Hello?"

"Uh, is this 432-8367?"

Tommy vaguely remembered that number so he said, "Yes."

"Are you Tommy?"

Now the angel was totally flummoxed. Who could possibly know he was here, call that number which he had made up earlier and get his *hand*?

"This is Jane Pierce. You left a message on our answering machine yesterday evening. We were asleep and this morning we had to get the kids off to school. It's the last day before break and... You said something about Deacon John?"

Tommy slapped his head, which would have smashed a real phone. Fortunately Marsha was not looking: she was old-fashioned and proper enough to afford him privacy. "Of course," he realized. This was the couple with the marital difficulties that the deacon had counseled.

"Oh, yes. Yes. Thank you for calling back."

"Is there a problem with Deacon John? We'd love to help. He is a terrific man. What can we do?"

"Uh, it's a little complicated to get into over the phone." Tommy had to say that because with the deacon issue now resolved, the angel did not know what else to say. Yet something told him it would be a mistake to let this lady go. Mrs. Pierce filled in the silence by saying she would be happy to meet him. She gave Tommy the address and asked if he knew where it was. Somehow he did, he did not know how, but he saw it vividly in his mind.

He said he could get there in...well, instantly, but that might raise eyebrows, so he said in half an hour.

"Great! We'll be expecting you. But is the deacon all right?"

Tommy assured her not to worry and he would explain it when he arrived. As he "hung up" (actually just closed his hand and pretended to place the phone back in his pocket) the thought nagged at him: "How the heck do I explain this away? 'Hi, the deacon was having a crisis of faith but I showed him a vision and he is fine now?' They'll call in the guys with the butterfly nets!"

Tommy did not dwell on his predicament long because Marsha interjected. "I see you have a prior commitment. I hope you do not mind, but I could not help but hear some of the call. By the way, that is some phone you have there. I could not even see it. It's incredible the strides they are making nowadays."

Tommy agreed. "It is, uh, a very new model. The latest my firm's R&D department has come up with."

So as not to tax this arthritic woman, Tommy offered to see himself out. Not before he bade Marsha a "Happy Christmas!"—which she returned in full measure.

"Believe it or not, young man," Marsha said, "you have made me one happy woman today. This visit was a Christmas present I will cherish and thank God for."

"As well we should," was Tommy's reply.

.   .   .

No sooner did Tommy walk up the drive to the Pierce's house than he had a warm feeling. For one thing, the yard was not garishly decorated with plastic sectarian holiday displays. Two large bushes on the lawn tastefully decorated with miniature white lights flanked the only bit of sculpture on the property: a nativity set. Baby Jesus was missing; that told Tommy this was a family of traditionalists. They would wait until the clock struck Christmas before placing the infant in His crib. As he looked at the Savior-less crèche, Tommy recalled something Dad used to say when driving past such a scene. "For now Mary and Joseph are adoring the grass."

"You must be Tommy," Jane said as she opened the door with a welcoming smile. Tommy was hoping his luck would turn. "You're Deacon John's friend?"

Tommy acknowledged that he was. Jane ushered him in and beckoned the angel to sit in one of the comfy wingback chairs in the living room. This room was also tastefully bedecked with a generous Christmas tree. There were a plethora of presents beneath the tree.

"Honey," Jane called out. "Our guest is here."

Tommy heard, then saw, a fortyish man come down the stairs. He held out a wide hand. "We're happy to greet any friend of the deacon. We owe him a great debt." After introducing himself as Alex, Mr. Pierce sat on the small sofa next to his wife. He held her hand in his and the affectionate squeeze he gave her hand was noticeable.

"Excuse me, but Deacon John told me he counseled you over...marital issues," the angel remarked pleasantly. "But you do not seem at all like a couple that is in need of...uh, I mean..."

Alex smiled and Jane laughed. "It's all right," Jane said. "Our problems weren't exactly front-page news, but they weren't a secret, either. We were headed to divorce court."

"May I ask why? What happened?"

Jane sighed deeply. "Life happened. We got so caught up in the merry-go-round that we forgot what was truly important."

Alex interjected. "I allowed myself to become defined by work. I was up to five cups of coffee a day. Let me tell you, you give Corporate America the opening and they will work you twenty-four/seven. All the talk the HR idiots spout about quality of life is just something they believe they need to say. It is not a deeply held conviction. The only thing deeply held in the corporate bosom is the mother's milk of unlimited profits."

Jane said she also worked for a big corporation and seconded the notion. "No matter how well you perform, the bosses want you to surpass the goals next year, and the growth goals were insane."

Alex nodded. "It's like if Bryce Harper hit seventy home runs in a season, the owners would tell him he'd better get eighty next year or he's fired. Then after that, ninety, a hundred and so on. Pretty soon there wouldn't be enough at bats in a season to meet the accelerating objectives."

Alex explained that his company gave annual reviews, rating every exec on a one-to-five scale, five being the best. "So by donating both body and soul to getting a five, you know what it meant?"

Tommy shook his head.

"An extra five or six grand in pay raise. Big deal. The cost was too great."

"We were too exhausted for—for each other," Jane said.

"Believe me," Alex added, "after five cups of coffee a day, you get so wired you need a coupla' glasses of wine to settle down just to be able to sleep. There is no time or energy for anyone else. What's more, our nerves were frayed."

"We fought like cats and dogs," Jane said, "which may be a slight disservice to angry cats and dogs everywhere. But we did fight a *lot*." She put special emphasis on the word "lot." She added that the kids were neglected. Their oldest even got caught drinking beer behind the school gymnasium. "Instead of dealing with the root cause, we bickered some more," she said. "Played the blame game with each other."

Alex explained that it got so all the passion blew out of the marriage, like air escaping from a balloon.

"Living with each other got to hurt so darn much," Jane told him.

"We pretty much decided, actually yelled, that we'd had enough and would go to our respective lawyers to get out of this horror show."

Tommy noted that they did not, however.

"No, we didn't," Jane agreed. "My mother, who lives in Baltimore, is very religious. She goes to church every day. She begged me when I told her we were splitting up to give it one last try. She pleaded with me to go see a priest."

Alex said they even fought about that. He had felt it was the stupidest waste of his time. In the end he gave in just to silence his soon-to-be ex and get on with his life.

Tommy noted that they saw Deacon John, not a priest.

"Have you met our pastor? He would win the world's or-neriest cleric contest."

Tommy nodded. "I've met him. I understand."

"So we went to Deacon John. I did not exactly know him, but he always seemed approachable."

Tommy was curious. "What did he say to turn the mess around?"

"He did not say anything preachy or anything like the advice one might expect," Alex told the angel. "Good thing, for that crap would not have worked with us at all in the state we were in."

Jane said the deacon began talking about his own wife. How he had lost her and how he still carried "this incredible burning torch for her," is how Jane put it as Alex listened in agreement. "When I saw how pure his love for his late wife was and how that love defined Deacon John, not the pursuit of material goods…"

"I think each of us realized at the same time how deeply we had been committed to the other at one time," Alex jumped back in. "That we had lost that special something because we had begun to follow false prophets. I even said something to the effect, that I would give anything to have that kind of love again."

"That's exactly what you said, and when you did, I just lost it. I broke down in tears." Jane's eyes were again moist in the retelling. She wiped at them. "Next thing we knew, we were in each other's arms, kissing and crying…and our lives changed forever."

"It has only been a few weeks since we met with Deacon John, but we both have the feeling this is forever," Alex said. Jane picked up the thread, telling Tommy they were like new-lyweds—and that she expected the euphoria to last. They now had the fortitude to weather any storm on the horizon.

"But you are not here to listen to us," Alex said. "In your message you spoke of a problem involving Deacon John. What can we do?"

Tommy gave the *Readers' Digest* version of the story. When he got to the part about how the deacon had forestalled being at his daughter's deathbed in order to provide succor to Jane and Alex, Jane exclaimed, "That poor man! Oh, if only we'd known!"

Stepping in quickly to assuage any guilt, Tommy explained the deacon had undoubtedly sensed the depth of the Pierces' problem and known it could not wait. It was his decision, not a failing on their part. From there he led them through the deacon's crisis of faith and his determination to leave the church. "My original plan was to enlist you," Tommy said, "as well as other parishioners, to go to Deacon John and testify to his good works. To persuade him of the value of his current station." Before husband or wife could volunteer, Tommy told them the unexpected had happened in the time between the angel's call last night and this moment. Deacon John's heart had mended.

"That's wonderful!" Jane said. "But how?"

Tommy looked at her carefully. She later would say she felt his eyes pierce through to her soul. "John believes he saw a vision. Of his daughter safely enthroned in heaven."

"Probably delusional," Alex said, "but the mind, and religion, work in mysterious ways. Well, whatever works. I'm glad the deacon is better. He is a fine man."

"The mind and religion are not the only things that move in mysterious ways," Tommy corrected.

Alex looked puzzled by the angel's comment until Jane helped him. "I think Tommy means the Lord. The Lord moves in mysterious ways. Perhaps He sent a sign to the deacon."

Alex was about to say something but Jane hushed him. "It could be. Who is to know? The important thing is that Deacon John has been healed."

"True enough," Alex responded.

Tommy said he was sorry to have bothered the Pierces, but it had all happened so suddenly, "and I felt I owed you an explanation."

"Oh pish-tosh," Alex said, "you have nothing to apologize for. We would have been only too glad to help. As a matter of fact, as part of trying to refocus our lives, we have been trying to decide what we could do in the true spirit of Christmas." He motioned to the many gifts under the tree. "We clearly are not hurting. My bonus was not at last year's level, after my declaration of independence and with this recession, but it was nevertheless substantial. As much as we want to do for our kids, especially after the terrible turmoil they had to endure this past year of our, uh, crisis, we would still like to tangibly demonstrate that Christmas is about more than material goods."

Jane said in the absence of any better idea, they were going to make a generous donation to some charity. "The problem is, just giving money seems sort of cold. Not the strong statement we wanted to make to show the children."

"The other problem," Alex chimed in, "is we don't know which is a worthy charity. We were thinking of the one that donates doctors' time to correct underprivileged kids with cleft palates. You know, overseas, in countries where the malady amounts to social leprosy. Jane was partial to that idea. As good as it sounds, however, I read somewhere that to really cure the defect a number of surgeries is required and the follow-through may not be there. So the poor kid ends up as badly off as before."

"Then you hear of horror stories about charitable organizations where the lion's share of the contributions goes to line the pockets of the fund administrators," Jane pointed out. She paused as if unsure whether she should add her next comment. "We are reluctant to give to the Church, though as you know from the Deacon John connection we are Catholic. The problem is we are not comfortable that any gift would not just find its way to pay off on the pedophilia scandals."

"After all this time," Alex said, "we're not convinced the Church has turned over a new leaf. Every so often more scandals and cover-ups keep popping up in the news. "There are too many instances to be able to say it is the media's anti-religious bias. Why, I remember reading that idiot former cardinal of New York retracted his apology to the child molestation victims and said the Church had done nothing wrong."

"So what do we do?" Jane asked.

"All of your points are valid," Tommy answered. "The best advice I can give you is what a wise friend told me. Don't over-think it. Just follow your heart."

Alex commented that sounded like the sort of nugget an old person could give you.

When Tommy saw young Jesse in his mind he was about to point out their error. Except he quickly realized that based on when Jesse was born, he was now over two thousand years old. So Tommy said they would not believe how old the wisdom was.

"It sounds nice," Alex said, "but what exactly does it mean?"

At which point Tommy's heart inspired him the second time. He snapped his fingers. "I just love being able to do that."

Jane and Alex exchanged glances, for finger snapping hardly seemed a momentous occurrence. Tommy did not catch their look. He went on.

"It must have been my night for running into hard-luck cases." He told them about Edward's plight.

Husband and wife exchanged another glance, this one more meaningful. "I do not have hiring authority for my company, and it does not sound like he has the skill set for my line of work," Alex said, "but we would be happy to give you the check we were planning to send to some charity. To help this poor guy bring some gifts home to his family."

Tommy released so deep a breath he later learned the emotional force was felt in the hereafter. "That would be wonderful!"

Jane tugged at her husband's sleeve. "Honey, I have a better idea, just a teensy tweak of yours. Why don't we do that tangible gift-giving we had hoped for?"

"Sure. What do you have in mind?"

Jane nodded toward the Christmas tree. "Our children are too old for Santa," she told Tommy. "So we don't have to go through the charade of hiding the presents until they are asleep on Christmas Eve. That's why we put them under the tree as soon as they are purchased and wrapped. They become decorations as much as gifts."

Tommy commented that she was very efficient.

"A blessing and a curse," she said. "Part of our problem I freely admit was not being good about the spontaneity thing. Anyway, honey," she looked back at Alex, "we and the kids do not need *all* these presents. Truth be told, we probably overdid it. Why not set aside a few gifts from each pile for that family? From what Tommy has told us, it sounds like their children are roughly the same ages as ours."

Alex nodded. "I like it. Instead of giving money."

"No," she corrected him. "In *addition* to giving money. Come on. This family is really poor. It would mean so much to them."

Alex again nodded. "And to us. Okay. Let's pick out some presents and give it to this fine gentleman..." Jane cut him off.

"Remember my mother's old saying? 'A gift without the giver is bare.'"

"You want us to play Santa personally?"

"Uh-huh. The children, too."

Alex smiled. "I like it!" He kissed Jane sweetly on the cheek. "I knew I'd married someone special."

Jane nodded happily. "Yeah, you're right," she said, giving him a playful punch on the shoulder.

"The kids only have a half day of school," Alex told Tommy. "Christmas break starts today, and they should be home in an hour. Can you give us directions to this, uh, Edward's place?" Alex smiled. "I feel really good about this."

"Me too, hon," Jane said.

Alex explained that he always took the full day off on Christmas Eve. "In case there are last-minute things that need getting done for the holiday," he said. "This year we have everything in order. But I'm glad I was here to meet you. It's almost like you were heaven sent."

"Imagine that," Tommy replied, and all three laughed.

Jane said speaking of that, she had noticed something curious when Tommy had left his phone number. "That number, 432-8367, do you realize it spells out something?" she said. "It spells H-E-A-V-E-N-7."

"Imagine that," was all Tommy could say, and again the three laughed.

✦Four✦

After Tommy provided directions to Edward's house, Jane and Alex invited him to stay for some early lunch and wait until the children got home from school. Tommy politely begged off, saying that he was not hungry just now. Which was true enough. Angels have no need for material sustenance; theirs is of a spiritual nature. So he spoke accurately when he told the Pierces he had no appetite. He just omitted that he *never* had an appetite.

The other thing was that while there was no time in heaven, time was a transcendent fact of life here on Earth, and Tommy was acutely aware of the dwindling time he had left. So he was driven to take even the slim hour to do what he could. The angel did not have anything specific in mind. He just intended to walk the streets and see if anything of good cheer befell him. As it turned out, "befell" was the operative word.

Tommy was so absorbed in his thought process he paid no heed to where he was heading. As he stepped aimlessly off the sidewalk he heard a loud honk and the squeal of brakes—and turned just in time to see a car plow smack into him. The amazing thing was the car, a Lincoln Town car, passed right through him, as if he were made of air. It then screeched to a halt and a man jumped out of the vehicle. "Mister!" he said. "I am so sorry! You came out of nowhere! Are you all right?"

Tommy said he was fine. That it was entirely his fault for not looking where he was walking. "Mommy always tells me to look both ways," he said, which the driver in his panic did not seem to notice as a childish response for an adult to make.

The man stammered. "But…but…I swear I saw my car hit you! How is it you are unhurt?"

Tommy said he must be mistaken. "I guess I jumped out of the way in the nick of time," he added, telling another of those little white lies he deemed acceptable to protect his angelic mission.

The man was greatly relieved though still visibly shaken. Tommy talked to him to make sure he was calmed down before getting back behind the wheel.

"You are a nice man," the driver said. "Other people would already be on the phone to their lawyer to sue me." He introduced himself. "I'm Angelo."

Tommy remarked on how impressive an auto Angelo was driving.

Angelo explained it was part and parcel with his occupation. He was a professional driver. Had his own car service.

Tommy asked if Angelo was on his way to work now.

"Shortly I have a call, but not this instant. Sadly, I wish it were otherwise. There is not much work these days."

The angel frowned. "You mean competition from the taxi cabs and Uber drivers?"

Angelo said no, that was not the problem. Unlike in the big city, there was no well-developed taxi industry in suburbia. Most residents owned their own cars. Actually most families had more than one auto. Angelo's business was centered on two events. Transporting passengers to and from major venues, such as family outings or couples going into the city for a night on the town, and business trips to the airport. Things like that. Things that required a more luxurious car than a yellow cab…or greater ease than the customer's own car. The problem was not competition, though there were other car services. As Tommy had heard countless times during his brief stay, the problem was the recession. With the economy in such a sad state, people were cutting back on frills. Using a car service seemed to be frill number one.

To make up the shortfall Angelo had taken to riding the streets as if he were a cabbie, trying to pick up random fares. He also slashed his prices. He was getting by. His family would not starve. But much belt tightening was required. As an example, he said, their washing machine had broken and they couldn't afford to replace it. Besides, the repairman had said the machine was so old and shot as to make any repair economically impractical. So Angelo's wife, Maria, had taken to washing the family's laundry by hand in the bathtub. "We get by," Angelo concluded, "but if I could get my Maria a new machine for Christmas it would be the answer to my prayer. Still, we have it so much better than others. God provides, you know."

"He does," Tommy said, smiling. "But how did you know? Did God speak to you, too?"

Angelo looked puzzled. "No, I just know it. Are you sure you didn't hit your head or something on my car?"

"Oh, great is your faith," Tommy remarked.

"I try. My family is well enough off for now. Our needs are simple. What's important is that I have a wonderful family and we love each other. The other things..." he made a dismissive wave of his hand, "like the washing machine, they will come."

Angelo glanced at his watch. "I might as well get to my assignment. It's my only call of the day." He turned to leave, then thought better of it. "My call is at the hospital. A businessman I've assisted in the past. He's not a pleasant man, but he's well off and is a paying customer. If you are going downtown to anywhere near the hospital, I would be happy to drive you. No charge, of course."

Tommy had no need of wheels or any need to revisit downtown, but something in his heart told him to keep Angelo company. Partly to be sure his own thoughtlessness in stepping off the curb had not so unnerved Angelo as to inflict a real tragedy later on. An angel could never be responsible for causing harm. So he gratefully accepted Angelo's offer.

On the way they chatted, actually Angelo did, about his family mostly. He and Maria had two children, a son and a daughter. Both grown up now. The son would be visiting his fiancé's family for Christmas; Angelo and Maria's daughter and her new husband would be home for the holidays. "We, especially my Maria, we are so hoping for a grandchild now. Maria talks non-stop about it when she is with Veronica, my daughter, but all my daughter says is soon. Some day.

"'By then I will be dead,' Maria laments."

"It is a good problem to have."

Angelo agreed, then commented it was like his next and only customer for the day, an unpleasant customer but a paying one. "A good problem to have," Angelo said. "It beats the alternative."

"Unless the alternative was for the man to be a pleasant and paying customer," Tommy opined.

Angelo grimaced. "From your mouth to God's ears."

"Exactly," Tommy said, to which it was Angelo's turn to frown. There was no time to pursue the thought, however, because now they were at the hospital.

Angelo parked outside the emergency room entrance. He was illegally parked, so he asked if Tommy could do him a favor and wait with the car. "If a policeman or a security guy comes, move the car. Just circle around."

"Uh, sure." Tommy gulped. After his recent escapade with combustion engines, he had sworn off driving forever. Forever intentionally being a long time in his estimation.

Fortunately no one pestered Tommy, and Angelo was pretty quick. In no time at all Tommy saw his new friend come out the hospital exit accompanied by two people: a portly, middle-aged, grumpy-looking man in a wheelchair, his cast-encovered leg propped up, and a nurse pushing the wheelchair. The nurse looked unhappy as well, but unlike the patient's angered look hers was more of a "woe is me" expression.

Tommy got out of the car to see if he could assist in time to hear the nurse muster in her most chipper voice. "Here we are, Mr. Talbott." She handed him a pair of crutches as he struggled out of the chair. "Hope we have a nice day."

As he slowly stood, Talbott growled, "*We* are having a frickin' incredibly bad day!" He grabbed at the crutch, almost toppling over in the process. Angelo stepped in to keep him from falling. The nurse made brief eye contact with Tommy and, rolling her eyes, turned with the wheelchair back into the safe confines of the hospital.

Talbott clearly did not have the knack of using his crutches yet and Angelo had his hands full trying to help the overweight man move forward, so Tommy stepped in. He might have expected a thank you for his efforts, but what he heard instead was, "Get in the car! We may need help when we get back to my house!" Even if Tommy had the slightest inclination to be off, Angelo's deeply imploring look convinced him to go along for the ride.

The silence in the car was uncomfortable. Tommy turned from his front-seat passenger perch and asked what happened.

"The world is filled with effin' morons, is what happened!" The man was breathing heavily and sweating. Tommy did not know if this was due to the effect of his recent injury or of carrying too many pounds. He suspected it was not the former, for Talbott seemed the type whose anguish was perpetual. The large man went on. "I was driving to the office this morning when this stupid kid, how the hell do the imbeciles at Motor Vehicles let these kids get licenses, hit a patch of ice and plowed right into me. Completely wrecked the front end of my car. It's probably totaled. Left me with this busted leg."

"Well, it was an accident." Tommy spoke calmly.

"The kid was an idiot! He ought to lose his license and have to pay for my insurance premiums which will undoubtedly go up!" Talbott broke the ten seconds of intervening silence with, "No car now, so I will have to rely on the car service here. Why should I have to pay for that? My company has used you in the past, haven't we, driver?"

Angelo kept his eyes on the road. "Yes, sir."

That Talbott did not know Angelo's name did not escape Tommy. Talbott continued to vent as he repeated, "Why should I have to pay for a private driver?" Tommy tried to point out to the man that the added car service cost should not be too onerous from a personal perspective, inasmuch as his company was bearing the cost.

"Hell! I'm the company! I own it!"

Tommy refused to give up. He hoped to draw out some spirit of kindness in this fellow. Talbott was still raging, however.

As bothered as the man was by the loss of his car, he was in a lather over his own lack of mobility. "We're closed tomorrow and the day after for the holiday, but after that how am I supposed to get to work as a cripple? Time is money! Where do I go to get reimbursed for my lost time?"

"Surely you can maneuver on the crutches, once you get used to them."

"Look at me," he growled. "With two good legs I have a lot of bulk to heft around. Business lunches and dinners are critical to what I do. I can't help it if I've put on some weight. And I have never been athletically inclined. So I am not all that coordinated. I'll never get the hang of these frickin' crutches. What's worse is my house is real nice. The entryway is quite impressive, but that means stairs. Big, steep steps. I'll never get down them. The doctor said I'll be hobbled on these things for six weeks. No way can I afford to be out of the office that long, even with the computer and my mobile."

Why didn't he get someone to help, Tommy volunteered.

"Like who?" Another snarl.

"Your wife?" Tommy ventured gingerly. "Uh, are you married?"

"Hmph. Twice. Paying both bitches a hell of a lot in alimony. Oh, yeah, I've got the scars to prove I've been shackled. Anyway, as much of my hard-earned funds go to 'em, neither one is going to lift her well-manicured finger for me. No kids, either."

"Friends?" Tommy offered.

Talbott looked at him as if he had three heads. "I am a business man. No time to make nice to people."

Tommy said he was a little confused. Wasn't kindness good business in addition to being the right thing to do?

"You in the business world?"

Tommy admitted that he was, but not in the sense intended.

"What I thought. It's hard to understand if you're not part of it. It may be cliché but it's true: it's a dog-eat-dog world out there. The competitors all want to make you break out in assholes and shit yourself to death. I've been successful because I screw them first."

Tommy remarked that the last statement seemed a perversion of the Golden Rule.

Talbott shifted his great bulk in his seat. "God, I already need to scratch my leg but I can't. This is going to drive me crazy." Getting back to Tommy's point he replied, "Listen. There is no room for that religious crap in the business world. For me the real Golden Rule is, 'Those who screw their enemies first get the gold.' Especially in my business."

What business was he in, Tommy wanted to know.

Entertainment. Talbott had his own talent agency, one of the more significant ones on the East Coast. "I can go toe to toe with any of those faggots in La-La land," he boasted.

It still seemed to Tommy antithetical that lack of kindness engendered strong business relationships. There was no percentage in pursuing this, however. Nor was there time, for Angelo was pulling into his passenger's drive.

It's a good thing Tommy had tagged along, for Angelo could never have gotten the businessman safely into his home on his own. Talbott himself was next to worthless. To be fair if Talbott had put half of the effort into his crutches that he did into his incessant cursing as they inched along, Tommy's assistance would not have been needed.

As soon as they were inside the house, with Talbott flopped onto a sofa in the TV room, Tommy commented on what a small world it was. He had been surprised to see that this man's palatial residence was only three doors down from Marsha's. Except for the elderly lady's simple abode, the rest of the homes in this neighborhood leaned toward what Tommy's parents would have called McMansion status.

Talbott was not taken by the coincidence of Tommy's making the acquaintance of two neighbors in so short a time. Rather he reserved special venom toward "that old bitch."

Tommy was taken aback. He remarked that Marsha had seemed to him to be a sweet old lady.

Talbott said the neighborhood had grown up long after Marsha had been in her home. "We've tried to get her to move out or at least renovate her hovel. It's such an eyesore and has a depressing effect on property values. She does not belong here."

"But it's her home. She was here first," Tommy retorted.

"So were the Indians, but we kicked their asses off the entire continent. Look, there is no law of squatter's rights. It's survival of the fittest. That old woman does not fit in this upscale neighborhood."

The angel asked what the businessman would have Marsha do. Talbott's response chilled Tommy. "Let her just go off and die." Tommy wondered if, aside from his brief run-in with Lucifer himself, he had ever been in the presence of such pure evil. He said a silent prayer that grace find its way into Talbott's diseased soul. That was probably a mission for another angel, another time. This would be too arduous an undertaking, for Tommy had too much closing in on him as the clock ticked toward Christmas Day. He and Angelo started to leave when the angel paused. He asked Mr. Talbott, solely out of curiosity, if he might be Jewish.

"God, no! Why would you ever think that? It's all I can do battling with those hymies! Especially those smartass Jewboy lawyers from New York!"

The remark was consistent in its wild inappropriateness. Tommy explained the reason he'd thought Mr. Talbott might be of the Hebrew persuasion was because there was no sign of Christmas in the house. No tree or decoration of any shape or form.

"I never bother with any of that garbage! All Christmas is is an excuse for the marketers to milk the dumbass public for all they are worth."

"No," Tommy said, "Christmas is a celebration of God becoming man."

"Oh, please!"

Once outside Angelo exhaled. "A very evil man."

"Indeed."

"You know, I have driven him on and off for the last six years and in all that time he has never given me a tip. He pays the bills, usually late, but never anything extra. Hey, let's not speak of sad things. It is Christmas, after all. Thank you for your help, Mister Tommy." Angelo embraced the angel with a hearty, "Merry Christmas!"

"And to you too, my friend," Tommy said.

Angelo asked if he could drive Tommy someplace.

"I appreciate it, but I only have a short way to go and I could use the walk."

"I understand. The crisp air will clear your head after having to endure Mr. Talbott. Here." Angelo produced a business card. "If you ever need me. No charge for you, my friend."

Tommy felt good. "The merriest of Christmases to you, Angelo."

"Every Christmas is a good one. I so love this time of year."

The angel marveled at how he had just met two men. One was materially rich but tone deaf as to the meaning of the Nativity while the other was struggling financially but held its spirit within him each and every day of the year.

Angelo got in his car. Before he pulled out he glanced in the rearview mirror to make sure he didn't almost run over Tommy again—and saw nothing! He craned his neck, looking all about. Then he got out of the car and did a three-sixty. One second Tommy had been standing there, and the next he was nowhere to be seen. It was as if he had vanished into thin air!

.　　.　　.

At that very instant Tommy winked back into existence. He blinked and looked about him rapidly. "Hmm," he groaned. He had missed his goal, Edward's home, but this time by only about two blocks. Not too far and easy enough to walk. "Well, at least I am improving," he said and set off merrily on his way. Tommy's sense of direction may still have been a tad flawed, but his timing was impeccable. He arrived at Edward's house just as the Pierces were pulling up. The doors flew open and Jane, Alex and three children with about a dozen gifts emptied out of the minivan. The children looked a little tentative.

The proud parents introduced Tommy to their children, who were polite but seemed unsure as to this strange odyssey they were on. This was certainly something their peers at school were not doing. As Tommy greeted each child, Jane whispered in his ear that the youngest, Jenna, was very shy. Yet the little girl stared at Tommy intently…and then flung her arms around him and hugged him warmly.

"Jenna!" Jane called out. "What are you doing?"

The little girl looked at her mother. "It's okay, Mommy. He's not like a stranger or something. He's an angel!"

Tommy was surprised but maintained a poker face. Jesse had told him things like this happened sometimes. "Why do you think Jesus was so partial to children?" Jesse had asked. Children often had better powers of perception than adults when it came to the spiritual realm.

Jane laughed indulgently. "Oh, honey, no. He is a very nice man, though."

"No, Mommy," Jenna insisted. "He's not a man. He's a little child, like me! And an angel!"

Jane's eyes narrowed as Tommy placed his hand on Jenna's shoulder. "Why don't we go ahead?"

At the doorstep to the run-down home Jenna had another suggestion. "Let's all sing Christmas carols." Jane looked to Alex, who shrugged. "Why not?"

Tommy looked at the oldest child, Alex Jr., and sensed the boy thought this was a little odd but was well-mannered enough to hold his piece. Tommy could tell he would go along, albeit reluctantly. Until very recently Alex Jr. had undoubtedly been convinced his parents would be getting divorced and the family would split up. Then it suddenly all turned around and Mom and Dad became as lovey dovey as could be. He'd probably decided his parents' good cheer was the best gift he could ever ask for. Having to go along with this rather dorky Christmas caroling and visiting a poor family, was likely considered a welcome price to pay.

Jane rang the doorbell. A woman Tommy assumed was Edward's wife, Elena, answered, and the small group broke into a spirited rendition of *Hark, the Herald Angels Sing*, which struck

Tommy as ironic. Elena did not have to call her family. Edward and their three children came at the sound of the happy voices.

The youngest of Edward's children in her joy cried out the obvious: "Mommy! Daddy! Carolers!" The poor family had heard of such things and had seen them on the idealized life scenes depicted in made-for-TV movies, but nothing like this had ever graced their doorstep before.

After the herald angels had hearkened, Edward beamed and told his wife, "This is the very nice man I told you about." He was looking right at Tommy, who wondered what man Edward was referring to. Tommy's self-image was still of himself as a child. Just as it took getting physically used to his new body, so too was the mental adjustment taking some time. At last the angel realized, "Oh, he means me!" and stepped forth to offer Elena his hand. Introductions were made all around, and Elena invited their guests into her family's very humble home.

Edward and Elena did not know what to make of the gifts. At first they assumed the packages were a prop of sorts, lending an air of Christmas authenticity to the carolers. However, when the family Pierce laid the gift-wrapped boxes under the simple tree, Elena realized what they were and said, "You are so generous, but we cannot accept your...charity."

Jane took Elena by the elbow gently and led the mistress of the house a few feet aside. "Elena, Alex and I have been through a very difficult period lately," she said. "I know you don't know us, but it would be a wonderful gift to us if you would accept these few things from our family." Elena's eyes welled up and she flung her arms around Jane, who also misted as she heard Elena croak, "God bless you!" Elena turned back to everyone then and apologized for how sparse a tree it was. Truly it was much like the Charlie Brown tree Tommy had seen in Marsha's old house.

Jane walked to the tree and fingered some homemade garlands made of green and red construction paper. It was clear the children had done this. "Oh, Elena," Jane exulted with evident sincerity. "It's beautiful!"

"It is all we can afford. A simple tree for so grand a feast."

Jane said, "Like God becoming man in a manger."

Elena lit up and offered everyone some snacks. She had just baked a batch of gingerbread and sugar cookies, which truly were the best the Pierces had ever tasted. Apple cider was passed all around and Edward proposed a toast. Despite his shabbiness, he seemed transfigured into a dignity that could not be superceded in terms of nobility of spirit. He proposed a toast to "our new and already dear friends…and to Tommy, our little angel!"

"Hear! Hear!" Alex said.

Tommy blurted out, "How do you all know?" and he could not understand when the entire group laughed.

In the corner Jenna whispered to her new soulmate, Samantha, "You can tell he's an angel. I never knew little kids could be angels."

Sam agreed and said, "He's a cute boy angel. I like him!"

For his part, Tommy's heart was soaring, especially when he noticed Alex surreptitiously hand an envelope to Edward. Edward was overcome for a few moments before he clasped Alex's hand in both of his and expressed his heartfelt gratitude. Edward also managed to sidle up to Tommy and thank the angel. "This is so wonderful!" he gushed. "We do not have much, but we do have love."

"Then you are rich beyond anyone's imagining," Tommy replied.

Tommy tried to excuse himself several times for he had urgent errands to run. Those of his Heavenly Father and that of his Earthly mother and father. It was just after noon and as much as the scene did Tommy's heart good, he had growing butterflies because of the enormity of his remaining tasks and the scarcity of available time. No matter how he tried to depart, however, Edward, Elena, Alex, Jane and their children would not hear of it.

The party lasted a while longer. More carols, more cider, more shared stories, much laughter, deepening intimacy and an abundance of good will. Then Jane and Alex said they should be off to allow Edward and Elena to get ready for their private Christmas Eve festivities, much as the Pierces would for theirs. Alex offered Tommy a ride but the angel declined. He stood outside, waving goodbye with Edward, Elena and children and he heard a clock somewhere toll one. Tommy whispered, as his lips moved but no sound escaped, "Jesse, help me. I'm in trouble!"

Almost instantly a shimmering mass appeared. It was Jesse in that half-you-see-him, half-you-didn't way.

Now Tommy's whisper was audible. "Jesse! Aren't you afraid they will see you?"

Jesse explained that Edward and his family could not see him. Their eyes were held fast.

"Tommy, do come inside," Elena coaxed.

"Oh, you go ahead," Tommy answered. "I would like a minute alone…to enjoy the outdoors."

When Edward and his family were back in the house, Tommy explained his predicament to Jesse. "I need more time."

"Of course you don't," Jesse replied. "You have hours still."

"But Jesse, that's hardly any time."

Jesse put his arm over Tommy's shoulder. "For an angel, that's like a decade."

Tommy was about to protest but Jesse bid him be quiet. "You are still thinking in human terms. Remember, we have no time."

"Tell that to them! Their clocks keep moving forward."

"It's amazing," Jesse replied. "When we are alive we dream of time travel, when all along we are travelling into the future, one second at a time."

Tommy asked how that would help him.

"It won't, but it seemed like a cool observation to make. Believe me. You have more than enough time."

"Jesse, what if I don't? What if I fail? Letting God down is not the high watermark for an angel."

"No, but it depends on how you fail. I messed up my first two tries out. First time I was supposed to visit Rome but my sense of direction was so far off I ended up in North America. Near what today is Detroit but then was just a Native American village. I ended up helping a band of Indians who were having crop difficulties. I failed, but in helping someone it was not a total loss.

"The second time, I was supposed to help save a group of people from being tortured to death. Remember Nero?"

"You mean the Roman emperor who persecuted the early Christians? You were there? But didn't Nero fiddle while Rome burned?"

"Tell me about it," Jesse recalled glumly. "I gave him the violin. Thought music would soothe the savage beast." The guardian angel scoffed. "It did not work out as I had planned."

"Oh, boy. What happened? Did you get in trouble?"

"I did not distinguish myself, but since I had good intentions and ushered a number of the people safely through the inferno, I got another chance. It was a while, however."

Tommy asked what Jesse's third mission to Earth had been about.

"The third time did turn out to be the charm. But how is not important now."

Tommy pleaded with Jesse to tell him about it, please, and Jesse relented.

Jesse got a faraway look as he told the story. "As you know, we are usually sent to the region where we lived because we have familiarity with the place and its customs. That's why you are here in upstate New York and not in China."

"I don't speak Chinese."

"Exactly," Jesse answered. "Anyway, I was sent to the Piedmont."

Tommy looked at his guardian angel quizzically.

"In northern Italy," Jesse added helpfully.

"So you're Italian," Tommy said.

"Well, in my time, it was before the unification of Italy. So the country was a collection of city-states. I actually think of myself as more Piedmontese than Italian. I was sent to help a particular soldier. He was from a well-to-do family and at the time, the soldiers served the nobles."

Tommy asked when this occurred.

"We are talking thirteenth century. Did you learn about the emergence of modern Europe in your history classes?"

"Not yet." Tommy paused and added, "Actually not ever, I guess." He began to grin broadly. Jesse could not see what was so funny so he asked his charge.

"No more school," Tommy replied.

Now Jesse smiled at the remembrance. "Yes, I used to get the same goofy grin when I had first gone to heaven and realized every day was what I suppose you would call a 'snow day.' By the way, you will learn about European history and lots of things over time when you are back upstairs."

"There are classrooms in heaven?" Tommy was beginning to fear heaven was not all it was cracked up to be.

"No, silly. By talking to the people who made the history."

"Won't that take a long time?"

"You have eternity."

Tommy agreed. "Good point."

"The point I was getting at," Jesse continued, "is that the feudal system was breaking down, but the large nation-states were not yet in place, so local barons, dukes and nobles ran what passed for government, including maintaining armies for peacekeeping purposes. Sort of a police department and an army rolled into one. It was still a less civilized time, however, and the soldiers pretty much did as they pleased. That included stealing to supplement their wages, womanizing and a lot of partying. A *lot* of drinking. Pretty much day in and day out."

"Why didn't the people stop them if the police were doing the robbing?" Tommy wanted to know.

"Do you realize how hard it is to stop someone who is heavily armed and backed up by a gang of like-minded associates? One of the soldiers was not into robbing and thievery. As I said, he came from a merchant family and was well off, so he did not really need the money. Besides, deep down he had a good heart. But he was into the partying scene. Big time.

"As a matter of fact, the first time I met him, he was sleeping off a powerful drunken state. He woke suddenly and almost ran me through with his sword."

Tommy asked if Jesse had been afraid.

"No. We're angels, Tommy. We cannot be hurt by things like swords."

"Oh, right. I keep forgetting."

"That will change in time."

"Why did the soldier want to hurt you?"

"He thought I was taking his apple."

"Were you?"

"Of course not. We don't need…"

"Food," Tommy finished. He added, "It seems a little extreme to want to kill someone over an apple."

Jesse shook his head. "It is extreme to kill someone for *any* reason. You are right, of course. But he was in the midst of a tremendous alcoholic binge."

"Wow. Does drinking affect people that badly?" Tommy was surprised. Once when he was very little he had mistakenly taken a sip from his father's glass. It was an amber color and Tommy thought it was ginger ale. It was not, however, and the beer had a horrendous taste. Tommy would never understand why adults drank such awful-tasting beverages. Jesse told him alcohol, beer and otherwise, affected humans in different ways, none of which were good.

That added to Tommy's confusion as to why people would intentionally put such harmful things into their bodies.

"It's complicated," Jesse said, eager to get on with his story. "When the soldier came to, he never even realized what he had done. To stay close to him, I introduced myself as a new recruit."

"You became a soldier?"

"Uh-huh. Figured it was best to be in his unit and try to set an example. When I got back to heaven I was actually commended for coming up with the idea of enlisting."

Tommy asked what Jesse did when the soldiers misbehaved.

"I did not go along. I made a point of sitting off by myself and reading the scriptures. There was a small pocket volume I carried along in my knapsack that I would randomly pull out at such times. The guys would ridicule me for being such a holy roller. They were intrigued, however, especially about the little book. That was the second thing that earned me a heavenly commendation because of my creative thinking."

"Wait a minute. Archangel Michael rewarded you for having a little book? I know it was the Good Book, but what was so unusual about that?"

"Tommy, it was the thirteenth century. The printing press was not invented until 1453."

"Then how did you get it?"

"As they would say in your century, 'Duh'? Tommy, our sense of direction as angels is not restricted to blinking from place to place. We can travel to different times. Remember there is no time in heaven, so no barriers to us. So I just got it from the future and brought it back with me to the thirteenth century."

Tommy was impressed. "That was clever."

"Thank you. Anyway we fell into a routine. The soldier would go out with his other buddies and get stinking sick drunk, I'd stay and read scripture and tend to him when he came back. This happened day after day. For weeks."

"You're lucky. You had weeks for your mission."

"Oh, yeah? Be careful what you wish for. I began to despair of ever influencing the soldier to mend his ways. Fortunately my guardian angel cheered me on."

"*You* had a guardian angel?"

Jesse looked at Tommy. "I wasn't born a thousand years old." He continued the story. "Then I had a brainstorm. One night when the soldiers were drunk, we happened to be in a town where an old girlfriend of his lived. He was still sweet on her. Was she ever pretty. I can still see her face. Her name was Clare. I brought her to visit her old friend. When she saw him she was so disgusted. She slapped him, told him he was a disgrace and she never wanted to see him again.

"The next day, a commotion broke out in the town square. In front of the cathedral, which in those days was the center of town. A man was whipping one of his servants, who struck back. The soldiers were called in. I was first on the scene, probably because I was the only sober one. I intentionally jumped into the fray without my weapons. The attacker laughed at me and said I was powerless to stop him. Rather than back off, I told him I was armed with the mightiest weapon of all, the word of God."

"What did he do then?" Tommy inquired.

"He hit me."

"Well at least you could not be hurt."

"No, but no one knew that. Each time he hit me I just said I would keep turning the other cheek. Eventually he punched himself into exhaustion. At one point he actually fell from the force of the blow and his tired state. Then he did the strangest thing. He simply walked away, leaving me to the cheers of the townspeople. Clare was there and commented what a shame it was that all soldiers could not act thus.

"The first person to rush to my side heard her. It was my soldier friend. He told me I had accomplished more with non-violence than he ever had with his fists. The army was due to muster out to a neighboring town with whom our duke was waging war. The soldier, however, said during my altercation he had a dream, obviously a daydream, that told him the military life was not for him and he should return to his own people. So he did."

Tommy was surprised the army would just let a soldier desert. Jesse reminded him that the soldier's family was affluent. "Money talks."

"Then what happened?" Tommy asked.

Jesse shrugged. "That was pretty much it. I returned to heaven. You see, my mission was to turn him away from a life of indolence and violence. Once I did that, I knew he would find his way. Though how spectacularly he would do so, even the archangels had no way of knowing."

Tommy asked if the soldier, or rather the ex-soldier, accomplished some notable achievement.

"I'll say. Not right away, however. He went on a voyage of self discovery. Started reading his own book of scripture. Said he got the inspiration from me. Prayed a lot. Fasted. Made a pilgrimage to Rome. Eventually he believed he saw and heard God talking to him. This introspective period lasted a few years, after which he dedicated his life to the Lord's work. He had a tremendous impact."

"How so?"

"Tommy, the soldier was Francis of Assisi."

"Wow! That's why I saw him give you high fives when we were in heaven."

"Yes, we are kind of tight."

The little angel was impressed that his guardian had pulled off Saint Francis of Assisi. "The reason I shared the story," Jesse said, "is I also was concerned about timing. You are worried yours is too short. I fretted that so much time had elapsed I had missed the opportunity to convert Francis. As you see, however, it worked out and in the most mundane of ways. It's not like we sprinkle pixie dust or something. Just perform good works. That's all it takes."

"So what are you telling me I should do now?"

Jesse smiled at his charge. He also still saw Tommy as a little boy. "Keep doing what you're doing. Good works to all whom you encounter. The rest will fall into place. Above all remember what I told you before. Follow your heart. Do not overthink it. There is a reason why young lovers pledge their hearts and not their cerebral cortexes. See you soon." With that, the shimmering essence vanished.

Tommy walked to Edward's door and rang the doorbell. "They must wonder what's taking me so long," he thought.

However, when Edward opened the door he remarked, "That was quick. You only needed ten seconds to enjoy the great outdoors?" Before Tommy replied Edward said, "You are a good person but a little odd, I must tell you. From the window it looked like you were talking to the bush. It's a good thing it was not a burning bush. Then I would think you were Moses reincarnated, or some other spiritual messenger."

"What a vivid imagination you have," Tommy commented. He thanked Edward and Elena for their hospitality and said he really must be off.

Elena thanked Tommy again profusely for the kindness he had shown, including rallying the Pierces to help brighten Christmas in Edward and Elena's home.

Edward gripped Tommy affectionately by the shoulders. "Please, isn't there some way we can repay the goodness you have shown us?"

Mindful of scripture, Tommy told Edward and Elena to "go and sin no more."

"We have not the riches the Pierces have to share with a downtrodden family," Edward said. "Still I wish I could do something with my hands to help a person in need."

Suddenly Tommy had an idea. "Wait!" he said. Before he could express it, he carefully positioned his fingers just so—and snapped. "I have a great idea!" he said brightly. Since it was Christmas Eve, Tommy did not want to set Edward on a path that would consume too much of his day. He told Edward what he had in mind. Asked how long it would take to build.

From what Tommy described, Edward said he could do it in two hours or so. "Especially if I enlist you, Señor Tommy, and Elena and the children."

"Well, come on!" Tommy called. "We have Christmas cheer to spread!" Edward grabbed his tool box, Elena got the children dressed in their overcoats, scarves and gloves, and the small group happily set out.

✦ Five ✦

Marsha had just sat down by her Christmas tree to look at the ornaments depicting her daughter. In her reverie, the elderly woman started to doze. She smiled just before nodding off at how impressed that nice young man, Tommy, had been over these same ornaments that she had always treasured.

The old lady awoke with a start. She thought she heard a bang of some sort. As with most elderly people, Marsha's hearing was not what it once was, but thankfully her other faculties were fully functional. She thought she had heard the bang in front of her house. "Was I dreaming?" Marsha wondered. She closed her eyes for a moment. Sometimes when she settled her mind immediately after wakening, a dream would come back to her. As it did this time. She chuckled at the remembrance. It was of that nice Tommy she had met. In the dream he had suddenly sprouted wings and carried Marsha aloft to her daughter's just in time for Christmas. "Oh, how the subconscious plays tricks on us," Marsha thought, though she basked a second longer in the warmth of the dream. She was actually about to doze off again when another noise brought her back. This time from the rear of the home. This was not a bang, but a longer, scraping sound. Like something being dragged along cement. Since noise did not figure prominently in her dream, Marsha realized the racket must be real. She did so hope there were no intruders in the backyard.

Getting up from her easy chair, Marsha stretched to work out the creaks and cracks that inevitably settled in whenever she slept. Then she walked to the kitchen and looked out the rear window. There was no sign of anyone, friend or intruder. It was a simple backyard. Only a small garden to tend in the summer. Nothing appeared wrong until Marsha noticed what was missing. "Oh, dear!" she placed her hand to her mouth. What a strange thing for someone to take. The old wood pile Herb had gathered for eventual use as a gazebo was gone. Marsha thought to call the police, then thought better of it. While she felt somewhat violated, and saddened that this last remembrance of Herb was gone, she reasoned that it was only wood after all. The police had more important things to do, so Marsha made no movement to use the wall phone. That was the only telephone in the house. She did not see the need (nor had she the financial wherewithal) to purchase a mobile phone with its costly and confusing plans.

Marsha was about to let the matter drop entirely when she heard the first noise again. Yes, it was coming from the front of the house. In fact it sounded like it was right at the front door. She crept toward the front door, pausing at the bath to pick up her hair dryer. It was vaguely gun-shaped, so Marsha figured it might be useful if she had to scare any intruder off her property.

Now as she stood at the front door, she fretted that she had never replaced it with a door that had a peephole or small window. Marsha placed her ear against the door. She could only make out one voice, and some sort of tapping. Later she would question her judgment in not in fact calling the police, but for now Marsha flung the door open. The sight was stranger than the dream she'd had of Tommy as an angel bearing her through the air. Her "angel," Tommy, was there with a man who wore carpenter's pants and appeared to be of Hispanic origin. The man seemed startled when Marsha threw the door open. He had a tape measure out that he dropped at the sight of the barrel of a hair dryer pointed directly at him.

"Uh, I have already shampooed and dried my hair today," he spoke as he retrieved his measuring tool.

Tommy jumped in and told Marsha they had not meant to startle her. They had knocked but there'd been no answer. Tommy introduced Edward and his family and told Marsha that Edward was a carpenter. "He's going to build you a ramp so you can go in and out of the house, even when your joints act up."

Elena stepped forward. "Merry Christmas, Señora," the young, attractive woman said.

Marsha was flustered. "Dear, dear me. Why…how wonderfully kind of you all." She wiped at her eyes. "Thank you. And Merry Christmas to you as well!" She quickly put the dryer on a stand next to the door. "Please do come in. I bet these young ones would enjoy a batch of brownies I made earlier. And some milk. Come in, before you work."

Edward and Elena's hearts were full. To be able to give back when they had so little was a heady experience. As Tommy looked from the couple to the old lady, it was hard to tell who was more filled with joy. Marsha was as upbeat as Edward and Elena. This was her second set of visitors in the same day. For one who went weeks without a caller, this was a red-letter day indeed. As they used to say when children played neighborhood ball, "Tie goes to the runner." In this case Marsha was the runner. That is, the happiness edge went to her over Edward and Elena for the simple reason that in addition to her joy over hosting company, the company had come to do a good deed for her. While Marsha and her friends chatted happily, Tommy cast occasional anguished glances at, appropriately enough, Marsha's grandfather clock.

The little angel mulled over the possibility of stopping time itself. If he could stop Earth's rotation on its axis, just maybe time would halt, allowing him to speed up completion of his assigned tasks. The problem was Tommy had not had many science lessons in his few years in school. Was it rotation or revolution he needed to halt? Moreover, if he stopped Earth's movement, in addition to stopping time (which he presumed would be the case), would harmful side effects ensue? From the dim recesses of his memory he called up an old PBS show his dad had watched. The documentary had depicted the sudden stoppage of Earth on its axis. The computer simulation showed people and objects hurtling off into space. If Tommy had to scurry off to retrieve the many fallen-away life forms, he would never get around to accomplishing his mission. If, on the other hand, he guessed that it was Earth's revolution around the sun he should stop, was there a risk that half of Earth, the stationary side facing the sun, would be baked while the other hemisphere would enter a new ice age? Talk about unleashing unwanted collateral effects! Beside all that, time stoppage somehow seemed to Tommy to be against the rules of the game. To win by cheating was to lose. So the angel resolved to stay but a short while longer and then make his way onward. This group was getting along so well, there was nothing more Tommy needed to do here.

"Tommy?"

"Huh?" He had been so absorbed in his ruminations he had not realized Marsha was talking to him. At last he snapped out of his reverie to hear the elderly lady proclaim that Edward reminded her so of her departed husband. His skill in carpentry was only part of it. It was Edward's gentleness of spirit that struck home.

Marsha told Tommy she was so very happy. She thanked him for this second visit. "I never thought I would see you again after this morning."

Actually, Tommy told her, this was almost the third time their paths had crossed. He told Marsha about his freak encounter with Mr. Talbott, her neighbor three doors down.

Marsha made a face. "You spoke the truth when you said it was a 'freak encounter.'" She went on to tell Tommy that Mr. Talbott was one of the meanest people she had ever encountered.

Tommy said he thought perhaps it was because of the tycoon's recent run of bad luck. His accident, his broken leg, his inability to maneuver his own stairs in to the house, the same predicament befalling Marsha.

"I am tempted to say it serves him right, all the years he has tried to get me kicked out of my own house," the sweet old woman said. "However, this is Christmas. What would Our Lord say to hear me speak in such a way?"

Tommy said he did not think the Lord would hold it against Marsha. An occasional fit of anger was allowable. "He did overturn the moneychangers' tables, didn't He?" The angel added that he thought, after making the point via an ostensibly angry display, Jesus would wish the best for His enemy.

"And so shall we," Marsha said confidently. "Not a further disparaging word about Mr. Talbott. In fact, a Christian wish that he be of good cheer this season."

"He is alone," Tommy observed. "Hard to be motivated to have good morale when there is no one to act as cheerleader." Marsha gave him a curious look, then busied herself with plying Edward and Elena's children with more brownies.

In short order Edward said that he best get on with his Christmas Eve chore. "It is not supposed to be for Christmas *next* year," he quipped.

"If you do not need me, I really had best be going," Tommy confided.

Edward assured him that would be fine. "I could do this in my sleep, let alone with Elena and the children to help."

Edward picked up his level and Tommy was about to head off when the angel was brought up short by a piercing "No!" He found it surprising that so loud a command could come from one so frail as Marsha.

"No," she said again. "I think it best you do not build the ramp. Not here, I mean."

All turned to stare at her.

"I will do a workmanlike job," Edward insisted. "It will not look like some slapdash construction."

"Oh, my dear, it's not that," Marsha said with a laugh. "It's just that I suddenly had a better idea. There is someone who could so much better benefit from your good work," she said. "Someone who could not only make more use of it, but for whom it might help stir his heart." She asked Edward if he would bring the lumber three doors down—and build the ramp for Mr. Talbott.

"Yes, I can do such a thing, but what of you, Mrs. Marsha?" Edward asked.

"Oh, I shall get by. At my age it's not like I need to go out on a regular basis. And I have resolved in my mind that I will visit my daughter's family for New Year's. Please. Go and help that poor Talbott fellow. If we melt his Scroogian heart, then I have done my Christian duty."

Tommy said he would help transport the lumber, then had to be off. It was three o'clock.

As soon as they laid down the lumber at the Talbott residence, they heard a loud bang at the door. Coming from the inside.

"What was that?" Edward asked.

Tommy, who'd been just about to ring the ornate doorbell near the door, perceived the sound had come from a crutch being flung at the door. While he, Edward and Elena exchanged glances, a voice from within hollered, "What the hell are you doing? Get that wood off my front porch!"

Tommy introduced himself to the closed door, raising his voice to be heard. He explained they would like to build a ramp to give the businessman easy access to his driveway. "It's a gift from your neighbor Marsha a few doors down." This announcement of good will was greeted by silence. The angel decided to wait a few minutes in case the irascible executive had any further outbursts. There being no further commotion, Tommy and Edward starting sorting the lumber in preparation for the ramp's construction. After just a few moments, however, three police cruisers drove onto the street. While one went directly to Marsha's house, two stopped in front of the Talbott residence.

Within twenty minutes Marsha, Tommy, Ed and Elena and their children as well as five police officers stood in the massive front hall of Talbott's home speaking to him, who sat in the middle of the hall in his wheelchair, cell phone in hand. "Officers, either you arrest these people right this minute or I will call the mayor and the chief of police to file a complaint and provide them with your names and badge numbers.

The officers' faces went blank, and one assured Talbott that wouldn't be necessary. "Please just let us know your formal complaint, sir," he said. Talbott waved dismissively toward Tommy and Edward and Elena as well as the children. "This motley group trespassed on my property, created an inordinate racket truly disturbing the peace and defaced my property," he cried.

The officer in charge nodded and turned to dismiss three of the other officers. "We can handle this," he said, turning a stern gaze toward Talbott. As the officers left through the home's massive front door, a newcomer knocked on the open door and stepped inside. The man, who looked to be Talbott's age, introduced himself as a judge who lived down the block. "I saw the police fleet outside and thought I might be able to offer some assistance," he said. He looked at Talbott. "We've been neighbors for years, Talbott. I'm not sure if you're aware of that."

"Judge Miller! Of course I knew you lived down the block. Just don't get out to neighborhood functions much. Your assistance is definitely needed as this officer here doesn't seem to think my complaints are of much concern. Wait, let me call my driver in case you feel the need for us to move this to the courthouse."

"The courthouse...?" Judge Miller began, but Talbott already had Angelo on speed dial. "Driver!" he barked into his phone. "I need you at my residence at once!"

Tommy turned to the police officer and the judge and explained the chain of events and how he and Edward and his family had come to be at Talbott's house with a load of wood. Marsha, Edward and Elena all corroborated the angel's story.

"That's nonsense!" Talbott interrupted. "They dumped that wood onto my porch and scraped it all up!"

Judge Miller spoke. "So on your ride home from the hospital today you told this gentleman and your driver that your livelihood depended on being able to enter and exit your home?"

Talbott nodded but then pointed a shaky, pudgy finger at Marsha. "But there's more! This woman is trying to worm her way into my good graces so I will cease my campaign to get her evicted. Her hovel is an eyesore and it hurts all our property values."

The judge peered over his glasses. "You would evict one of our neighbors...on Christmas Eve?"

Talbott nodded. "She is an economic menace to the neighborhood. As for him!" He was pointing now at Edward. "It is clear he intends to bilk me by charging some exorbitant amount for building this ramp they all seem to think I suddenly need.

"No, sir," Edward said, adamant. "I seek nothing for what I have done other than God's good grace. There will be no bill. There never was an intention to charge you. Then it would not be a gift."

"Well, then you probably see it as a ploy to force me to give you a job!"

The judge looked back to Edward, who said, "It is true I am looking for work, but I do not know what Mr. Talbott does for a living. So when I undertook this task I had no expectation of seeking employment from him."

The judge sighed. "It seems to me that all these people tried to do was an act of Christian charity. There is no crime in that.

"On the other hand," the judge added, glancing at Talbott, "there is also no law against being a bullying, insensitive ass. If there were I would lock you up for sure." He shook his head, then pulled off his glasses and rubbed his eyes. Finally he addressed Tommy, Edward and Elena. "Unfortunately, despite your good intentions, there is the matter of trespassing."

Marsha, who had been mostly silent, asked if she could speak. The judge gave her leave.

She addressed Talbott. "Every one of us had a simple motivation: to share a good work with you and this…this is how you repay kindness? Your mother must be ashamed of you!"

"My mother died when I was eight," Talbott retorted. "You leave her out of this! You have no idea what she's thinking!"

One of the group did know what the departed Mother Talbott was thinking, however, and he spoke up. Tommy told the misanthrope, "Your mother still loves you, but she does wonder how the heart has grown so cold in her Mikey-Mike."

This last brought Talbott up short. He stared for a long while at Tommy. "How…how did you know that? No one alive knows that's what my Mama used to call me."

Talbott closed his eyes, and then he turned to wheel himself a few feet away from the group. Tommy approached him. When Talbott looked up he whispered, "Who are you?"

"Just a messenger of hope."

Talbott's eyes narrowed. "This is some kind of trick. It must be. If you really have inside information about me specifically, then what was the last Christmas present my mother gave me?"

Tommy looked with compassion on the anguished soul. "Michael," he said, using Talbott's Christian name, "times were harsh when you were young. Your mother was an immigrant and after your father died, she did the only work she could find, as a cleaning lady. She got you a collection of science fiction books you always wanted. About a young astronaut in a secret corps in the early days of space flight. Mike Mars it was called."

"Yes!" Talbott exclaimed in a whisper. "There were eight in the series. They went out of print quickly. I...I still have them. I never knew how Mama scrimped enough from her meager wages to purchase the set."

Tommy smiled beatifically. "She sold her winter coat."

"No! She told me she was too hot and only wanted to wear her worn sweater for the winter months."

"Yes, that is what she told you. Love is sacrifice, Michael... and not letting on that sacrifice has been made."

"Oh, God! She must have been so cold."

"Not where it counted. In her heart."

Talbott put his face in his hands.

No one else in the front hall knew what the hushed exchange between Talbott and Tommy was about, but they were all anxious to conclude the affairs at hand. "Mr. Talbott!" Judge Miller called out. "Please rejoin us. Sadly, the law does not account for good wishes. So if you insist on pressing charges..."

"Wait!" Talbott turned his wheelchair quickly to face the group once again. "That will not be necessary, your honor. I withdraw all claims," he spoke quietly. Marsha, Edward, Elena and even the judge and policemen smiled.

"A wise decision," the judge said. He and the police officers beat a hasty retreat, and Tommy and his small group quietly made to follow. They were halted, however, by another cry from Talbott.

"No! Wait! Please come back!" The group did so, tentatively.

Looking directly at Edward, Talbott asked if the carpenter could build two ramps. "One for my home," he said, "and one for Marsha's."

Edward said he could, but he would need more lumber. "And I do not have any money to buy lumber," he said. "Besides," he added, "the lumber store is closed by now."

"Then," Talbott said, "the day after Christmas, buy what you need and send the bill to me. No...no, better yet. Edward, is it? Spell your last name for me, Edward." Talbott reached into his jacket, pulled out a leather checkbook and furiously wrote out and tore off a check. "Here! For the materials and for your labor as well."

Edward's eyes bulged when he looked at the check he'd just been handed. "This is too much," he said, offering to give the check back.

"No," Talbott said, shaking his head. "Any excess is to tide you over until...until...," he glanced upward as though trying to remember something...or flip through a mental Rolodex. "I have a contact at the Stephen Colbert show. They can use someone to work on assembling and taking down their sets. The excess," Talbott indicated the check, "will cover you and your family until the Colbert crew comes back from their break. That will also give me time to make the calls and get you placed."

Edward slowly grinned. "You are serious? This is not some trick?"

"No, I am done with tricks. This is real."

Elena hopped up and kissed Talbott on the cheek, causing him to do something he had not since adolescence. Talbott blushed.

"Thank you, Mr. Talbott," Edward stammered, still in shock over the size of the check he held.

Talbott hesitantly offered his hand. "It's Mike."

Edward grasped the proffered hand warmly. "Mike!"

Suddenly the assembled group turned at the sounds of a knock on the still-ajar front door. Tommy smiled as Angelo entered.

"My driver!" Mike Talbott exclaimed. "You've been waiting outside; I forgot I called you."

Angelo shot a quizzical look toward Tommy, who simply shrugged with a smile.

The businessman turned back to his checkbook and wrote another remittance. "Here," he said, thrusting this one in Angelo's direction. "This is a long-overdue gratuity and a fee to cover an important task for you, if you are available right now. It should only take a few hours."

Now it was Angelo's turn to be staggered by the sum handed to him.

"Yes...yes, sir."

"Good. Angelo, I would like you to please drive Marsha here to her daughter in Colonie."

Marsha stared at her neighbor. "How...how did you know my daughter lives in Colonie?" she asked.

Mike blushed again. "I...uh...may have had a private investigator do a little research on you, to see if there was something I could use to help convince you to move out."

Marsha's stare quickly evolved into an angry glare.

"I know, I know!" Mike exclaimed. "I was remiss. But at least I can now use that information to help you. Please accept my offer as an apology of sorts."

Marsha shook her head. "You are a piece of work, neighbor," she said. "But thank you, your offer to pay for my ride to see my daughter and her family is very generous."

Mike beamed. "Well, go on! Shoo! All of you have a wonderful Christmas. I've got a lot to think about while you do."

He winked at Tommy, who bent to shake the older man's hand. Marsha did as well. "I think right now your mother is very proud of her son," she said. Then she and Angelo filed outside after Edward and his family, all of them grinning as was Talbott, who simultaneously had tears in his eyes.

Talbott gave Tommy a questioning look.

"Yes," Tommy said, smiling in that angelic way. "Your mother says this is her real Mikey-Mike."

"Whoever you are, what can I do for you?"

"Nothing, Mr. Talbott."

"Mike."

"Nothing, Mr...Mike."

"Surely there must be something."

"Not for me directly. But there is a young man, a violinist, playing at Saint Anthony's tonight at the midnight services. He is quite exceptional. If you could give him a listen. That's all I ask. Assuming he is as good as I think, perhaps you..."

"If he is good enough, I will get him a recording contract."

"As long as you listen, then our debt is paid in full," Tommy told him.

"I am not a Catholic, however," Michael said.

"Do you go to any church services?"

"Not in years."

"Then it really does not matter. You will be welcome at Saint Anthony's without being coerced into joining up."

. . .

Outside Tommy was surprised to see Angelo standing by his town car with Marsha waiting in the front passenger seat.

"Please, Mr. Tommy. Come out of the cold for a while," Angelo said as he regally held the door open.

Inside Marsha said, "We have been scratching our heads trying to figure out how you did it, but we are stymied. No matter. From all of us, a Merry Christmas to you, Tommy."

"Yes, dear Tommy, the very best of days to you!" Angelo added.

"And to you both as well," Tommy replied as he got into the back seat of the town car. "As for Mr. Talbott, it was nothing. All it took was a good word and following my heart."

"No, my dear," Marsha said. "It was more than that. You have a rather singular touch. What is it you do?"

"Oh, I work with people."

"That explains it," Angelo said.

"Not quite. What exactly do you do with people?" Marsha asked.

"This and that."

"Oh, now I see," Angelo said.

"Well, maybe you can explain it to me," Marsha told him. Casting a glance back at Tommy, she said, "You are quite the mysterious fellow. Goodhearted, but mysterious."

"My work requires it."

"Well, we mustn't pry," Marsha noted. "Before we shove off, I want to be sure: Do you have someone to spend Christmas with?"

"Oh, yes," Tommy answered truthfully, "I will be at a rather large gathering."

"But I distinctly recall your saying you would not be with your parents."

Tommy said that was correct. Where he was going his parents would not be able to attend. Suddenly Tommy had an idea. "Marsha, do you trust me?"

The fervent way he said it inspired such good feeling in Marsha.

"Implicitly," she replied.

"Then could I ask a favor of you and Angelo?"

At the same time both said, "Of course."

"Since you will be in Colonie, would you visit my parents? It should not take long. Just tell them…tell them I sent you with the message that I'm all right, they need not worry and I will be waiting for them."

"But of course," Marsha said as Angelo nodded eagerly. "But," Marsha added, "why don't you come along and tell them yourself?"

Tommy got a long face. "I…I cannot."

"Is there a problem, dear? Are you estranged from your mother and father?"

Tommy told her not in the sense she meant. His parents meant the world to him, but he could not see them. "I cannot explain why. It is a requirement of my job."

"How very odd. Perhaps you should seek out a new line of work."

Tommy said no, he was fulfilled in his present role. "Please. Will you do it?"

Marsha reached out and patted the angel's hand. "Why certainly. It just seems to me a son should be able to see his own parents on Christmas Day. What sort of job do you have?"

"Now I understand!" Angelo cried out. "You're a spy. CIA perhaps. You're on a mission and cannot let anyone who would recognize you compromise your assignment by revealing your true identity." Angelo was close, though of course he was unaware of Tommy's angelic nature.

Tommy pointed at the friendly driver. "Bingo. I do not work for the CIA, but yes, I am with a higher authority and my identity must remain under wraps."

Marsha said she still thought it odd but would respect Tommy's wishes and yes, she would deliver the message.

Tommy thanked the lady and the driver and reached for the door. "Before you go," Marsha inquired, "will we see you again?"

"Most definitely, but not for some time."

Angelo said he also had a practical question before Tommy left. How to find Tommy's parents in Colonie? Tommy gave instructions as best he could but they were convoluted. There were a lot of twists and turns in the small upstate town, and Tommy was not good at directions. Like most small children he intuitively sensed the way when driving with his parents, but he could not afterward describe the route taken with any particularity.

Angelo said he feared he could not follow such nebulous directions. To make matters worse, his GPS unit was malfunctioning. It was under warranty but would not be repaired until after the holidays. "I can find Colonie easily enough. The Thruway is well marked. And the local roads here I'm familiar with. But local roads hours away? No way."

"All right," Tommy said resignedly. "Let me try harder." He stuck his tongue out and rolled his eyes skyward as he thought.

Tommy tried several times to describe the way but it was no use and at last he gave up. "That's all right," he said. "You just go on. It is getting late. I'll find another way to assure Mommy and Daddy that I'm fine."

Marsha peered at her friend and was struck by his little boy way of speaking.

"No," she said. "I have a better idea. Why don't you ride with us? You said you could show us the way, you just couldn't describe the streets. So come with us. Besides, I would love the company for the next two hours or so." She looked to Angelo.

"Ninety minutes, max," he said with a smile.

Tommy thought it over. Then he nodded. "I'm in." To himself he said, "I am following my heart and not my brain this time, but the hours are almost gone. I sure hope you know what you are advising, Jesse."

They made a brief pit stop so Marsha could get her suitcase. Since she had originally expected to be visiting her daughter via the bus, she was already packed. She also had a few presents to bring.

After Angelo and Tommy had placed Marsha's things securely in the trunk, they hopped in, and the trio was on the road to Colonie.

✦ Six ✦

The happy group drove off into surprisingly light traffic. Angelo commented that it was on account of the lateness. With Christmas Eve about to fall imminently, anyone who was visiting family or friends most likely already was at hearth and home. That, and the drawn-out nature of the holiday. Contemporary culture may not celebrate the twelve days any longer; indeed as soon as the presents are opened and dinner had, most trees come down, the carols are stilled for another year, and the fight to return or regift gifts begins in earnest. However, many people take advantage of the bracketing holidays of the Nativity and New Year's and the Saturday-Sunday combo twining them, thereby taking just a few extra personal leave days to end up with a week-and-a-half vacation. Not like Thanksgiving, he said, which is a mad rush from quitting time on the Wednesday before until the turkey comes out of the oven (and the football games begin).

Angelo was making excellent time. He punched it, figuring correctly, as it turned out, that even the state troopers would be on very reduced duty. As had become their habit, Marsha, who was still unused to enjoying the company of visitors, led the talking. She coyly tried to steer the conversation to Tommy's background, but the angel sidestepped her questions nicely. At one point Angelo asked if Tommy had anything to do with stopping terrorists. In the driver's mind, he could not shake the notion of Tommy as a real-life James Bond. Tommy told him he was sent to work with all people to combat hate, terrorist or otherwise.

"I knew it!" Angelo exclaimed.

It was clear sailing to New Paltz when Angelo suggested putting the radio on. The town car came equipped with satellite radio, not an extravagance of Angelo's design, but for the benefit of his pampered customers. There were five stations dedicated to holiday music, plus one Hanukkah channel. Of the five, one played classical favorites, which Marsha and Tommy expressed as their preference.

"The old music is so much better," Marsha declared, "compared to the modern carols. It is so much more...oh, what is the word?"

"Sacred?" Tommy offered.

"Yes. That is it exactly."

The station now played *Il Est Ne Le Divine Enfant*, which Tommy particularly enjoyed. Also some very old classical favorites, such as *Jesu, Joy of Man's Desire*.

"Oh, my, but how that takes me back," Marsha said. "One year Herb treated me to see the New York Philharmonic with Leonard Bernstein conducting, and that was one of the selections they played. It was divine."

"Well you ought to hear Bach conducting his composition himself," Tommy said dreamily, one of the few errors he made. It earned yet another curious glance from Marsha.

The station highlighted a few more recent classics, like *Silent Night* (only a hundred and fifty years young), and the three travelers sang along. As a matter of fact they sang the next half dozen carols that played, though when *Good King Wenceslas* came up, after the second line all three in the car had to resort to humming the tune. This caused much laughter, a fact Marsha commented upon.

"I feel so happy. No, better than happy. So energized."

"Spending time with nice people and nice music will do it every time," Angelo pointed out.

"Quite so," Marsha agreed. "However, I think it is more than that. There is something about young Thomas here that I cannot place my finger on. When you're in my presence, Tommy, I feel so much better. Even my joints seem to be healed. It's as if there is a power emanating from you that cures all in its path. Physically as well as spiritually. I still cannot believe how you reached the heart of Mr. Talbott. What was it you two were discussing just before his conversion?"

Thinking fast Tommy said, "Don't you think Christmas just brings out the best in people?"

With that, Marsha and Angelo led into a riff about Christmases past, sharing their favorite memories. "My all-time favorite Christmas was the year my daughter, Melanie was five," Marsha said. "She still believed in Santa at that age, of course, and Herb and I really doted on our only child. We bought a mini-swing set. One of the Fischer-Price plastic kinds. It was grand. I can still see it now. A red frame, blue seat and yellow slats to hold it all in place. It said easy assembly on the box but Herb and I were up until four Christmas morning—cussing the so-called ease of assembly.

"The next morning we were awakened by Melanie's excited shouts. It seemed we had just fallen asleep and yet our little girl was up at six or so. She had peeked downstairs and had seen the packages and came bouncing on our bed as if it were a trampoline. 'Santee came!' she shouted with each jump.

"We were so tired but when you love that much it may not conquer all, but it surely defeats slumber and the three of us excitedly went downstairs." Marsha began laughing as though she could not control herself. "You know what? Melanie liked the swing, but she *loved* the huge box it came in. She spent practically the whole day cavorting in and out of the box. It became her secret place. I took leftover gift wrap and decorated the inside of the box. Even drew a false window for her 'house.' Herb later told me if he had known all she wanted was a box, we could have saved a lot of money. Oh, but we all had the grandest time! I still have much of it on film. Herb was quite the home movie buff. The old eight millimeter is getting worn, however. I fear playing it again will cause the slender filament to break."

"Oh, but it's no good to leave it to sit in a box," Angelo pointed out. "There are film companies that will transfer the old film to DVD. You should do that and give it to your daughter next year for Christmas. I'm sure she, her husband and your grandchildren will love it."

"Why, I did not know you could do such a thing. Thank you for the idea, Angelo. You are right. They will simply adore it!" She asked the driver what his favorite Christmas was.

"It's hard to say. They're all so good. The early ones when my parents took me to see Santa. Then when my Maria and I were first married. And yes, like you, having children brings out the best in Christmas and in Christmas memories." He thought for a moment. "But if I had to pick one…" The driver was stroking his chin.

"It would be the second year we were married. Maria was pregnant with our first child but there were complications. The doctor said he did not think she would carry the baby to term, and if somehow she did, the baby would not be normal."

Marsha commented on how awful that must have been. What a burden for the young parents to bear.

"Yes," Angelo said, "but I prayed, as I never have in my life."

"To Saint Jude," Tommy noted.

"Yes, but how? How did you know?" Angelo half turned in his seat.

"Uh, lucky guess? Saint Jude is the patron saint of hopeless causes, so it made sense."

Angelo continued. "A week before Christmas, Maria gave birth. To a healthy baby boy. Maria wanted to name him Angelo, Junior, but I insisted he be Christopher, because he was our Christmas baby. He is all grown up now and no sign of illness. That was the greatest Christmas ever. To have our first-born and after all that worry to have him healthy. I was as high as the angels that day."

Marsha commented on what a lovely story that was. She turned to Tommy. "What is your favorite Christmas memory?"

"I guess they were all wonderful, though I have not had so many to choose from. Probably last year, when Mommy and Daddy surprised me with a train set going around the Christmas tree."

Angelo glanced in the rearview mirror at Tommy.

"Last year?" Marsha said. "Are you a train aficionado?"

Tommy caught himself. "Oh, no. I meant the year I turned five. It's all still so vivid in my mind. I meant it *seemed* like it was last year."

That led to some discussion of train sets. "I do so love it when people decorate their Christmas tree with a train running. It is so homey," Marsha said.

Angelo said he liked the old large-gauge Lionel sets from when he was a child. In his version, the locomotive actually puffed smoke out of its stack, and there were passenger cars that lit up from the inside, revealing silhouettes of passengers painted on the windows. There was some talk of the relative merits of large gauge as compared to the H&O small-gauge trains. Eventually the group arrived at a consensus. The large gauge was preferable, but all train sets had their own unique charm, especially during the holidays.

Marsha related that Herb had set up a miniature race car set once. Another year a single monorail track they had purchased while in Disney World. "They were nice but not as, I don't know, traditional, as trains. After that Herb went back to the reliable choo-choos. Now of course I gave the old set to Melanie. At my age it is too much bother to fuss with the tracks and wires and all, and the grandchildren get so much more out of it in their own home anyway."

The conversation slowed as did the town car. There were warning lights in the far distance, causing what little traffic there was to back up. From his vantage point Angelo could see the other side stalled as well, courtesy of the rubberneckers. "You would think they'd never seen a blinking light before," the driver commented drily. "At least it won't take us too long. I can see once we get past this commotion it is clear sailing ahead."

"I wonder what the problem is," Marsha said. "I hope no one has been seriously hurt in an accident."

As they got closer Angelo told her and Tommy that it looked like a disabled vehicle. Fortunately not an accident.

Now Tommy could see the broken-down auto on the shoulder. The flashing lights were from two sources: a police cruiser that had stopped to control traffic and a roadside assistance vehicle. That was not all Tommy saw. The disabled vehicle's passengers were also standing along the shoulder.

"Well, at least they won't be late for Christmas," Marsha said as she noted the curious garb of the afflicted car's passengers.

"Why?" Tommy asked. "Don't the Amish celebrate Christmas?"

Angelo and Marsha stared at their friend.

"Those are not Amish, Tommy," Marsha said.

"Hmm. Last summer I vacationed with my family in Lancaster, Pennsylvania. We went to Hershey Park with its amusement rides and visited the Gettysburg battlefield. These people look just like all the Amish people we saw then."

Angelo said he thought the Amish rarely ventured outside Pennsylvania.

"Oh," Tommy replied. "Then they must be Shaker or Mennonite or some sect like that."

Angelo asked, "What kind of a spy are you?"

Marsha mildly corrected Tommy. "I believe they are Hasidic."

"Jewish?" Tommy said.

"Most Hasidic are," Angelo tossed back.

Tommy noted that inasmuch as Angelo was good with cars, they ought to stop and see if they could help.

Angelo protested but Tommy was adamant in his gentle way so the driver went along. They were making such excellent time and Tommy was not someone you could say no to, so Angelo abided his friend's wishes.

A few moments later Tommy struck up a conversation with the stricken family's father. It turned out they were from Monroe, where there was a large Hasidic community. They were on their way to visit relatives in Canada for a mini-vacation. Their preference was to be out of the country this time of year with the incessant Christmas reminders. Christmas in Canada was more muted, he said.

Tommy excused himself when Angelo beckoned him over. Angelo had been in deep conversation with the tow truck operator. "It looks like they blew their engine," he explained. "There is no oil whatsoever in the engine, so it likely overheated and seized up." The Hasidic father had happened over and said that his oil light had been on for the last few days. He'd intended to nurse it along to the Canadian border where oil was cheaper, he claimed.

Tommy asked what Angelo would need to fix it.

Angelo and the tow operator looked at each other.

"It's not like replacing a spark plug," the operator said.

"It's not fixable, not without a whole new engine," Angelo explained.

"Oy vey!!" the owner exclaimed. "Never should I have listened to my brother-in-law Menachem when he told me it was good to go to Canada."

"We all have in-laws, pal," the tow operator commiserated.

"A shanda," which means a shame, the Hasidic gentleman, now a little distraught, said, agreeing. At last he said he would call his uncle Moishe, who lived twenty miles away, and ask him to pick them up. Then he would arrange with the tow operator to tow the damaged goods off the road.

The policeman came over and told the group they had to clear the road now. "We can't clog up traffic indefinitely," he ordered in his stern state trooperish way.

"Could you be mistaken?" Tommy asked Angelo, who assured him in this case that was not possible. "Go see for yourself," he offered. As the group set to bickering over how best and how costly to remove the pile of junk, Tommy sauntered over to the open hood.

Looking about to be sure no one was watching, Tommy waved his hand back and forth once. He asked the tow truck operator to try to start the car.

The man was reluctant to say the least. "We've been tinkering with it for nearly an hour," he said. "It's hopeless!"

Tommy gave him a look and, despite himself, the man felt obliged to say, "Just to satisfy you, I'll do it."

Tommy thoroughly enjoyed the looks he saw on the faces of the tow truck operator, Angelo, the car owner and the policeman when the engine turned over on the first try. The tow truck operator flew out of the idling auto and said, "This is impossible! How did you do it?"

Tommy replied, "I jiggled a few wires and said a prayer."

"Mister, if you can bottle those prayers, I could make a fortune."

"The prayers have long been bottled, as you say, though if you invoke the Almighty's intercession for profit-seeking motives, your prayers will never be answered."

Suddenly Angelo exclaimed, "I don't believe it! The dipstick indicates there's plenty of oil!"

The Jewish family was all smiles as they surrounded Tommy. "This may sound odd coming from us," the father intoned, "but we mean it with all sincerity and respect for your beliefs." Then the large family, boys' peis curls bouncing and the girls' bonnets flapping lightly in the breeze, shouted happily, "Merry Christmas!"

Back on the road Angelo kept muttering, "First there was no oil, then there was." He knew of no way a burnt-out engine could be restored and the oil reservoir filled by jiggling some wires. His attempts to engage Tommy in further explanation were unavailing, however, so he let the matter drop.

They drove another twenty miles or so when signs indicated they'd reach a service station within two miles. Angelo said he was under a quarter tank and suggested they fill up now in case the gas stations closed for Christmas. "I want to make sure I have enough to get back for my family's Christmas celebration."

A voice behind Angelo said, "The ten virgins."

Angelo had seen and heard many strange things in his years operating a car service, but never did he expect to hear those words uttered. "Huh?"

Tommy explained it referred to the parable of the virgins. Five were wise and took enough oil to keep their lamps burning for when the bridegroom arrived. The five foolish virgins did not, and when they had to leave to replenish their oil, they missed out on joining the bridal party. "So we should be like the wise ones and get our gas before it's too late," Tommy concluded.

While Angelo handled the pump at the gas station, Marsha remained in the car and Tommy got out to stretch his legs. There was a mini-food court-type of building and Tommy stepped inside. At the entrance were a number of vending machines. One held an assortment of the always-glitzy but cheap toys that small children love. Oversize rings, creepy crawlers in tiny plastic pouches, magnets, things like that. Tommy gazed at the collection fondly. A man with his son, who was whining away, excused himself as he stepped past Tommy and inserted a coin. Not that the kid needed the gift. It was more to shut the ill-mannered brat up.

When the tiny toy clinked into the slot, Tommy craned his neck to watch with much interest as the boy began to finger the new addition to his trove. The man noticed Tommy's interest. "You must be a collector or something," he said.

"Aren't we all?" Tommy replied.

The man asked why didn't Tommy spring for fifty cents and get his own.

"Nah. I'm just looking."

"Probably a smart idea," the man observed. "After all, you can't take it with you."

"That's true. They would never let me back in with that stuff."

The father gave Tommy a quizzical look and quickly ushered his son back outside in case Tommy was a little off or something. As the angel walked outside, he heard a sniffling sound. Off to the side was a bench on which sat a woman close to the age of Tommy's mother. As Tommy strained to hear, the sound of her crying was unmistakable.

"Excuse me, Ma'am," he said, approaching the woman. "Are you all right?"

She looked up, tears having streaked her mascara as she wiped her nose from a pocket pouch of tissues. "I am worn to the bone!" she exclaimed between sniffles. Her story poured out of her. She was the mother of an eight-year-old boy who had his heart set on a particular gift for Christmas. It was one of those years when there was a "must-have" toy the manufacturer and retail stores had purposely under-stocked in order to keep demand higher.

"I waited on line earlier this week at four in the morning at my local toy store. They opened at seven. I was the fifth one in line and after standing in the cold for three hours, once they opened, it turned out they only had four of the things. I offered the man in front of me a hundred dollars to take his spot on line, but he just laughed at me.

"That was three days ago. I have been travelling far and wide to find it. Every store in a one-hundred-mile radius. This morning I heard an ad on the radio. The Toys 'R Us store in Manhattan said they were getting a shipment. I drove eighty miles, fought traffic in the city, had to pay forty-five dollars for parking and after all that, the clerk said the ad must have been mistaken. They were not expecting a re-stock until after Christmas. I am just so, so frazzled at this point!"

Tommy said he was sure her son would understand and would not want his mother to go through all these stressful steps.

"What do you know? You're not a child. I so want him to have the best Christmas ever! What will he think of me and of Santa if he does not get his one wish for Christmas? Oh, I don't know what else to do!" She wiped at her eyes some more.

Tommy tried to reassure the woman. She did remind him a little of his mother. Tommy knew his own mother would walk through coals exactly the same way for him. Still and all, it was only a toy. Christmas was about so much more than presents. Why didn't people see that? Tommy wondered if he had appreciated that before he lived in heaven, but he thought he had. He liked toys and getting presents, but his parents had always stressed the deeper meaning of things. So Tommy now tried to release the same nuggets of wisdom.

"You are very kind and I know everything you say is true," the woman told Tommy, "but it does not really help anything. It's just that I wanted to do this for him. He's a good kid. My husband and I would hate to disappoint him, leave him emotionally crippled on Christmas."

Now that really struck Tommy as rather severe. Not getting a hoped-for gift might lead to mild disappointment. Heck, life was full of disappointments. But to be emotionally scarred by lack of a toy? Ridiculous. There were so many other issues that were genuine causes of emotional trauma: illness or death of a loved one, as Tommy well knew, dysfunction within the family, job loss, natural catastrophe. The list went on. Losing out on a toy hardly seemed to rank with tsunami on the list of tragedies. Tommy very tactfully put it this way to the lady who said she understood, but...

Out of curiosity Tommy asked what was the toy that was all the rage. He had been out of pocket only a few months now but as he racked his brain, no super-duper toy came to mind.

"What planet are you from?" the lady looked up mid-sniffle.

"No planet. We are in a sphere all our own." Rather than seek an elaboration, the woman divulged to Tommy the particular holy grail of a toy. "Haven't you heard of the Magnetopulse?"

Tommy got instantly excited. "They've invented it! They really have?" It had been in the talking stages when Tommy's illness first hit, and he naturally lost touch of developments in the toy universe thereafter. Now, however, Tommy was beside himself. "Why didn't you say so?" he asked the woman. "That puts things in a whole different light!"

This particular toy was an outgrowth of the wildly popular show "The Magnetrons." The Magnetrons were childlike beings that were half human, half machine, the result of an eons-old experiment gone awry on the planet Magneto before its sun went supernova. The small remaining beings that escaped the planetary inferno somehow managed to find their way to Earth, where they used their inborn magnetic powers of super strength for good. Magnetrons were the latest in a line of child fads that in recent decades had included everything from the Teenage Mutant Ninja Turtles to the Power Rangers to the Teletubbies to everything related to the latest Disney movie.

In the show, the characters wielded a stick, part symbolic, part power source, with which they maintained calm in the universe. It was that which the enterprising toy manufacturer had developed. Unlike a lot of knock-off fad toy concepts, the Magnetopulse was fairly sophisticated. It used actual magnetic power to do things such as levitate mid-air. Justly it had earned its place as the must-have toy to be craved this Christmas.

Tommy's six-year-old mind temporarily lost its sense of balance, so excited was he over the news of the Magnetopulse. Grabbing the woman by the shoulders he cried out, "Leave it to me, Ma'am! The Magnetopulse should be in your trunk before this day is done!"

Her sobs were immediately transformed to rapture as she looked at the angel. "But how? How can this be?"

Before Tommy could answer he was being pulled in the other direction. "Here you are! We were growing concerned! We must be leaving!" Angelo called as he pulled Tommy along.

Straining against the powerful grip of his driver-friend, Tommy called back to the woman, "Be not afraid! Only have faith! Look in your trunk!"

The woman shook her head as she barely made out the last words of the rapidly receding Tommy. "Merry Christmas!"

She shook her head again and grinned at the eccentric kook she had just encountered. "Well," the woman smiled as she stood. "At least he made me smile and get over my panic attack. My Jeffy may have a spoiled Christmas, but I will try to do my best." She went off to get a French vanilla caramel latte before driving the rest of the way home.

Meanwhile outside Tommy begged Angelo for a brief instant more. "I have to do one quick chore. It won't take but a minute. Please, Angelo." The goodly driver had to relent for he had a commitment to Tommy's heart. Though he did make the angel promise to hurry it up. He also offered to help, figuring that was the best way to keep Tommy on the straight and narrow, for the fellow did have a knack for stirring up trouble wherever he went. Tommy said he appreciated the offer of help, but this could only be done in private.

On his own, Tommy instinctively knew whence the woman's car was, a sure sign his angel powers were nearing full maturation. There in the cold, with no one else around, Tommy pressed the palms of his hands firmly together, then slowly pulled them apart. As he did so, an object formed and lengthened with each bit of space that Tommy's spread hands transcribed...until at last what he held was a brand new Magnetopulse. "Wow!" Tommy exhaled. Unable to resist, the little angel took the toy on a trial run, smiling happily as he put the wand through its paces.

He could have gone on for hours as it was an addictive toy, but then he heard an echoing voice call out sharply, "Tommy!" Tommy knew it was Jesse though he could not see him.

"It sure is a shame you can't take it with you," he said, looking up.

"Tommy," Jesse's reassuring voice spoke out of the ether. "We are angels. We have powers that make the Magnetopulse seem like a toy."

"But it is a toy."

"You know what I mean. Now be off."

Tommy had adult form, but his mannerism was decidedly childlike as he said in slow, drawn-out cadence, "All right."

The little angel popped the trunk, using his angel powers, of course, and with a flick of his wrist produced a brand new manufacturer's box for the gift.

Just then the woman was about to leave the foyer of the food court area when she saw someone at the trunk of her car. She thought it looked like that nice but unbalanced man she had just met. She ran off to find a security guard. They would be too late, for by the time she and the guard arrived at her car, Tommy, Angelo and Marsha were back on the open road.

Jesse sensed her imminent arrival. Good thing too for, despite himself, Jesse had himself begun playing with and becoming absorbed by the Magnetopulse. Just in time, Jesse released the toy, sealed it back in its package with a wink, shut the trunk and blipped back out of Earthly existence. The last of his shimmering remains dissolved into thin air as the lady and the guard came on the scene.

"Yes, I tell you," she explained frantically to the guard, "I saw him tampering with the trunk. Oh, if he stole any of my other Christmas presents, why I will give you and the police a full description and if and when you find him I will press charges!"

She fumbled in her purse for her keys, a complicated process because of the habitual difficulty she had locating the tiny set of keys in her mammoth-size handbag, and by her nervousness, for truly her hands were trembling. Once she had the key chain it took two, three tries before she pressed the correct button to unlock her trunk. Flipping the trunk lid open, in a flash she saw all of her Christmas packages—plus a brand-spanking-new Magnetopulse!

"Oh…my…God!…OhmyGod, ohmyGod, ohmyGod!" Tears came again, this time not of sorrow but of joy, and shame that she had thought ill of Tommy. She flung her arms around the burly and bewildered guard and kissed him on the cheek. "Oh, isn't it wonderful! He put the Magnetopulse in my car! Oh, what…what an angel!"

The guard asked, "So, you do not intend to prosecute?"

He scratched his head and left the woman there in the parking lot, her arms outstretched, eyes raised heavenward as she cried out over and over, "Thank you, God! Thank you, God! Thank you, God!" The woman did not bother to look for Tommy, for she instinctively knew she would never see him again, though he had miraculously restored her faith in her fellow man, and in Christmas magic.

Meanwhile as Angelo's town car shot off the entrance ramp back onto the Thruway, Tommy crooked his head. He heard something distant, something only he could hear. "You're welcome," he whispered, which caused Marsha to turn and ask to whom he was speaking. Tommy, of course, simply smiled at her.

The remainder of the trip was blessedly uneventful. When they saw the exit sign for Colonie Marsha tensed in anticipation. Angelo asked Tommy how to get to his parents' home. Tommy glanced at Marsha. She looked so drawn after the day's events and he knew she was eager to see her daughter and family. The angel leaned over the headrest and whispered in Angelo's ear. The driver smiled and nodded.

Moments later Marsha was pleasantly surprised that they had gone to Melanie's house first. She offered to wait until Tommy's mission was done but he waved her off. "Besides, it will give you a chance to freshen up," he said.

"I could do with that," Marsha admitted.

In the driveway Angelo honked. The family within came out to see what was with the unknown fancy car. When Angelo held open the door and Marsha emerged, the two grandchildren raced over and hugged her around the legs, the whole family in giggles, the elderly woman included.

Marsha introduced Angelo and Tommy to her family, explaining their vital part in bringing her here. Melanie gave each a warm hug. "Thank you so much! You have made our Christmas so much brighter!" She invited them all inside.

When Marsha told them about Angelo's need to return to his family and that she still had to visit Tommy's mother and father, Melanie's husband, Jim, said he would be happy to drive Marsha and Tommy, leaving Angelo free to go. As the driver left, fortified by Melanie with several brownies and a thermos of home-brewed coffee for the road, Marsha thanked him profusely and gave him a warm kiss on the cheek.

When it was Tommy's turn to bid farewell, Angelo said quietly, "Perhaps not a spy. I think maybe you're a magician, no?"

The little angel smiled enigmatically. "Goodbye, Angelo. Now you have enough money for your Maria's washing machine. Merry Christmas!"

Angelo embraced him in a warm bear hug.

Marsha placed her presents under the tree, each one causing squeals of delight from the children and smiles of happiness from the adults.

"Wait!" Tommy said. "There is one more. I have a gift for the children as well."

"Oh, Thomas. You shouldn't have," Marsha said.

"I want to." Looking at the children he said, "But there is only one gift, so you must share."

"I know," the boy, Joseph, said to his little sister. "You get it Monday, Wednesday and Friday. I get it Tuesday, Thursday and Saturday. Sunday will be a day of rest."

"Deal," his sister, Mary, said as she put out her tiny hand.

From out of nowhere Tommy produced a wrapped box.

The kids blurted out in unison. "Mommy! Daddy! Can we open it now? Please!"

The trio of adults looked to Tommy, who nodded his assent. "I would like to enjoy their reactions."

The parents gave their permission and the children tore off the wrapping. To the utter astonishment of all in the room, except Marsha who did not really get it, the kids literally screamed when they beheld their very own Magnetopulse!

"We've been looking for this everywhere," Melanie explained, "but have had no luck."

"How did you pull it off?" Jim asked, obviously impressed by Tommy's ability to procure such a rare find and by his generosity in sharing it with a family he did not know. "It's as if you pulled it out of thin air."

"Ssh," Tommy said with a finger over his lips. "Don't tell anyone," and the group laughed.

It was now about eight o'clock. The vigil Mass for children started at nine. Jim suggested he run Marsha and Tommy to complete their errand, and then he would come back in time for the service.

By now Tommy had the feeling he might not accomplish his heavenly task, but he was no longer afraid. He had done his best. He would throw himself at the mercy of the Almighty, Who was all merciful, wasn't He? Besides, Jesse had gotten a second and even a third chance. It was critical to Tommy, however, that he at least salve his parents' sorrow. That could not wait.

In the family car Jim asked Tommy the way. The angel's hand went to his head as he had a sudden vision. "My parents are not home. They are…they are at the cemetery."

Jim asked how he knew.

"Jim, dear, don't ask," Marsha said. "Somehow he knows these things. Let's just go to the cemetery."

"Fine by me," Jim replied.

On the way, Marsha asked her son-in-law to make a brief pit stop. At Ellen O'Brien's. She was the local florist and a young friend of Marsha's from earlier days. It was after hours, but Ellen would not deny a friend. If they were going to a cemetery, Marsha's old word instincts demanded they bring flowers.

Marsha quickly explained all to Ellen, who lived above her shop. As expected, she was very glad to gather a generous bouquet for Marsha and she refused payment. She did dispense some advice however.

"It is most unseemly for a child, no matter his age, to be apart from his parents on Christmas," Ellen said. You must get them together."

"But Ellen, I promised."

"Some promises are meant to be broken."

"Oh, I do not know," Marsha shook her head.

"How would you feel if you were that boy's mother?" Ellen asked.

"Well, when you put it that way…"

Ellen looked carefully at her friend. "There is obviously some barrier that your new friend Thomas is unable to cross. It is your Christian duty, especially at this time of year, to help him overcome the hurdle. The angels would be proud of you, Marsha."

"Well my dear, you certainly have given me food for thought. He is quite the strange lad. In a good way, but there is a very mysterious aura surrounding him that I cannot place my finger on." With that, Marsha was back in the car.

Less than half an hour later they entered the church grounds. The cemetery was in the rear. Then they were at the gates of Mary, Queen of Heaven Memorial Gardens. For Christmas Eve, the gates remained open late and the floodlights were on. Tommy indicated the direction and Jim drove on as Marsha held her flowers. And the little angel swallowed hard.

✦Seven✦

Mary, Queen of Heaven Memorial Gardens was small, maybe a total of three acres. On the narrow blacktop, Jim had to take a right and a left, at Tommy's bidding. As soon as Jim made the second turn, Tommy urged him to stop. In the distance, probably two football fields away, Tommy could make out his mother and father, and his throat caught.

Marsha said she would be all right to walk that distance. The walkway was paved, and it was level. She told Jim to return home, get ready for the service and come back with the family. She would walk over to the church after this errand and wait for the family there.

Jim would have wished Tommy well, but the little angel was so absorbed in his own world, Marsha's son-in-law quietly got back in the car and drove off.

There was a grove of trees, so Marsha and Tommy were well concealed. Marsha tried one last time to get Tommy to reconsider and greet his parents in person. There were tears in the little angel's eyes. "If only I could, but there is a very legitimate reason why I cannot. Marsha, you must do this for me. Just tell them not to worry. That their son is all right. That I look in on them and think of them often and will wait for them."

Marsha's heart went out to her friend. She could tell he was hurting. She just had to help.

The old lady bit on her lip and agreed to deliver Tommy's message. She would attempt to persuade Tommy no further. She did ask if he would stay with her family for Christmas.

"I would like that as well, but I cannot. Actually I have to leave now. Right now. Goodbye, Marsha."

"Will I see you again?"

Tommy gazed intently at her. He reached out and stroked her wrinkled cheek. "Soon," he managed to croak.

The two embraced, a lifetime of love in that brief hug, and then Marsha turned away with her flowers and shuffled off.

Tommy started to walk away, then stopped abruptly. He had to see this. See Mom and Dad one last time and be sure Marsha delivered the message. Keeping to the tree line, for now it was important that Marsha see him no more, he crept closer until he was about a hundred feet away. Too far to hear, but he could observe. At that moment, Marsha happened to turn in his direction. She did not see him. "Whew!" Tommy exhaled.

Tommy's eyes were riveted on his parents. "Oh, Mom!" he whispered fervently. His mother was crying as she stood in front of the tiny grave stone with his father, who had his arm around her back and was stroking her shoulder, looking stricken. "Please don't be sad," Tommy prayed.

It was at that point that Marsha reached the couple, who appeared momentarily startled by their visitor. Tommy could see Marsha speaking as his parents listened. Then Marsha leaned over and reverently placed the bouquet on the tiny grave.

It seemed to Tommy that Marsha was startled now, but if in fact she was, she quickly recovered. Then the elderly woman did something odd, at least in Tommy's estimation. She looked up to the heavens for a long while. When she was done, she began speaking rapidly to the grieving couple with her. It seemed she even gestured at one point in Tommy's direction.

When at last she was done, Tommy watched his parents each take turns hugging the sweet old woman dearly.

Marsha then stepped up to the grave, put her fingers to her lips in a kiss and touched the headstone. With that she nodded at Tommy's parents and returned the way she had come, back to the church. On her return she did not see Tommy hidden among the trees.

Tommy's parents watched the old woman until she was gone from their sight. When they turned back, Tommy saw they were...smiling! "Yes!" he said quietly as he did a quick fist pump. "Thank you, Lord!" Tommy strained for one last look at the couple he loved more than any other. Then he turned to leave.

Since his back was to them, Tommy felt he need not slink amid the trees any longer. So he walked slowly along the pavement, for all intents and purposes just another mourner. He had not gone twenty feet when his heart stopped, at least it would have if he still had one, as he heard a voice he knew all too well call out, "Excuse me! Please! Wait!" He could not ignore his own mother. Nor could he run. Tommy figured he would not be recognized in his adult visage. So he took an exceptionally deep breath, steeling himself to remain calm as he slowly turned around...to see his mother and father quickly approaching him. A moment later they were standing in front of him.

His father began to speak as his mother stared intently at Tommy's features.

"Excuse me," Tommy's dad said, "but that lady said you brought her here so she could bring us word from our son. We just wanted you...uh, I mean, we just wanted to thank you."

Tommy was relieved and surprised that his own vocal chords were able to function. He said it was nothing.

His father spoke again. "She also said she wasn't supposed to reveal your role in this, but she..."

Tommy's mom cut in abruptly, which Tommy knew was unusual for her. "She's been the latest in a string of extraordinary events that have happened to us today."

"Well," Tommy said, working hard to get his words out. "The important thing is you not be sad any longer. Your son would not want to leave you that way."

His mother smiled. "We are at peace with things, at least now. Oh, we miss him so much, but we know he is well taken care of. In heaven with the angels. That comforts us no end."

For the first time Tommy smiled. "Good!" He seemed overjoyed, and his mother again gave his smile a piercing look.

"By the way," Tommy's curiosity was getting the better of him. "What sorts of unusual things happened to you today?"

His dad said that they'd been getting signs from their son, who died months ago.

"Signs?" Tommy asked.

"First we got a call from a deacon in a parish a hundred or so miles south of here. A small town called Nanuet. He told us he'd seen our son. That he was an angel now and had helped the deacon get over a major crisis of faith."

Tommy smiled in spite of himself. "So that made you feel better?"

"Well, of course it did," his dad answered, "but it wasn't necessary. You see, our faith is strong and we always knew our boy would be in heaven right away. Of course, to hear that he's an angel…well, I guess that does make us proud."

Tommy grinned. "That was nice of the deacon to call."

"Obviously our son touched him deeply," Tommy's mom said. "Then a couple called. Their last name was Pierce and they shared a similar story with us."

"We've had a lot of visitors and callers," Tommy's dad said, picking up the thread.

"An old businessman. His name was Talbott."

"A nice man named Edward and his wife, Elena, also called."

"Wow," Tommy said. "It sounds like Grand Central Station in your home."

"And you don't know the half of it," his father added.

Tommy looked surprised. "There's more?"

His mom smiled. "Not long ago a car service operator named Angelo called us from his mobile. He was in his car on the way back home. He also had a story about how our son reached out to his heart in a special way."

"You're forgetting the violin player," Dad told her.

"I'm not. I just hadn't gotten to him yet."

The two were all smiles, which did Tommy's soul good.

"The last two were the strangest and the most wonderful of all," his father said. "You tell him, dear."

His wife explained how a little girl knocked on their door that afternoon. "At first I thought she was collecting for a school fund or something, but she asked to come in and said she had something to show us about our son. Of course we let her in. At first I thought that might have been a mistake when she told us she was an angel."

"I assumed she was pulling our leg and was in no mood for that," Tommy's mom said, "when she revealed the most amazing thing of all."

"The girl, or angel, said she was the daughter of a deacon... the same deacon we had spoken to earlier. It turns out she had died recently, as a young adult, but had been sent back to Earth in the guise of a little girl. I did not know what to make of it. Anyway, she said angels were allowed to share one vision with their loved ones, and that our son had used his in comforting her father. She was so grateful, she used hers to show us a vision of our boy in heaven with my mother and a friend of his!"

Tommy's mom started to cry. "It's all right," she said. "I'm not sad. It's just that it was so beautiful. You see, all this has made for a wonderful Christmas. And I know I will start eating better and taking care of myself. I'm expecting another child, you see."

She began to cry again as her husband hugged her. "Hormones," he explained to Tommy.

Tommy's mother nudged his dad with a smile and disagreed. "No, not hormones. I miss our child so much but I am so happy at the same time. Is that crazy or what?"

Tommy said no, that was the power of faith at work. He also, reluctantly, said he had to be off.

"But we didn't tell you about the elderly lady, Marsha, who just left. That encounter was almost as strange as the angel's visitation," his father said.

Tommy stood rooted, anxious to hear what they had to relate.

"When she first introduced herself to us, she seemed perplexed."

"Why?" Tommy asked.

"She said she'd seen our son, but he was much too old to be the son of a couple as young as we were. And when she saw his name, Tommy, on the gravestone over there, she was taken aback, though I'm not sure why."

Tommy's mom started to say she thought she knew, but Tommy jumped in. "Well, when people get old..." he started to say, but his voice trailed off. He breathed deeply and summoned all his willpower to hold his emotions in check. "You good people take good care of yourselves. I really must go now." The last two words ended on a sob.

Tommy had walked about five feet when his mother's voice called out, "Tommy!"

Despite himself, Tommy turned.

Tears welled up in his mother's eyes as she held her arms out. "My little angel!"

Tommy flew into his mom's arms, and then his dad joined in the family embrace.

"How...how did you know?" Tommy asked.

His mom smiled through her tears. "No mother can ever fail to see her child, no matter how clever the disguise. We miss you so, but our lives are going on, and we are so very, very proud of you."

"Son," Tommy's father said through his own tears, "whether you became a doctor or an angel, we always knew you would be the best at what you did."

Tommy took it all in but then stepped back for a moment. "I'm so sorry I have to go. But listen. When my baby brother is sixteen…"

His dad cut him off. "We're going to have another boy?"

"And a little later a girl. Anyway, when my brother is sixteen, on April seventeenth of that year he is going to want to go for a drive. It will be shortly after he gets his license. Ground him! Do not let him out of the house! Otherwise there will be an accident that afternoon, a drunk driver, and you do not deserve to have to bury two children."

"Got it!" his father said.

"We love you, Tommy," his mother said.

All of a sudden a tremendous noise sounded from above.

"How very odd," Tommy's dad noted. "I've never heard thunder like that. What's more, we never get thunderstorms this time of year."

"It wasn't thunder, Dad," Tommy said. "That was meant for me. They're calling me home."

"Are you sure?"

Tommy nodded. "I am sure."

Tommy and his parents embraced one last time. When his mother pulled away she was smiling, but Tommy knew she was putting up a brave front for his sake. "Remember what I used to tell you, Tommy," she said. "Life is short and we will all see each other…"

"In the wink of God's eye," Tommy finished the saying. Then he backed away, his hand raised in a farewell salute. His parents held each other and waved as Tommy backed up, his physical form beginning to fade. He kept growing dimmer, as from his line of sight did his parents, until with one final backward step, he could see them no more.

✦Eight✦

Tommy knew he was back in heaven. Everything was so white and pure. The strangest thing, however, was how quiet it was. The place seemed completely deserted. As far as Tommy could see, which in angel vision is quite far, he saw no one. Not even Saint Peter was manning the pearly gates.

"Gee," Tommy muttered to himself, "did they up and leave and forget to tell me?"

"Hello!" he called out. It did not come out as a single hello, but rather as a long drawn-out echo.

"HELLO...HELLo...HELlo...HEllo...Hello...hello...

"JESSE...JESSe...JESse...JEsse...Jesse...jesse...

"MICHAEL...MICHAEl...MICHAel...MICHael... MIChael...MIchael...Michael...michael..."

It was quite an echo chamber, as well should be expected, for Tommy's voice carried to eternity and back.

The little angel sat on a nearby cloud to think. The rumble that had sounded like thunder to his parents had sounded angry to Tommy. "They must be mad at me," he said with a sigh. "I failed to do the Lord's bidding, to find just five people who had good hearts." Then a sinking realization struck him. "I also broke the cardinal rule of the cherubim. I divulged my identity to Mom and Dad." Tommy put his head in his hands. "Oh, nooo! Whatever will I do?"

He stood up and looked about. Was this to be his punishment? To be banished all alone for eternity? Tommy did not know if he could take this. But he might not have a choice. Was this why he was called back while he still had three hours left?

"Well, whatever is going to happen, I have to own up to my shortcomings, and certainly I have to apologize."

He walked, slowly, for he was dreading what would follow. When he came to the archangels' chamber he tried to get in, but the way was barred. Nearby was the throne room, where at least he could beg the Lord's forgiveness. Unfortunately it too was barred. A light sweat broke out across the little angel's forehead.

He searched the places where he had taken angelic instruction, played with Jesse, visited Grandma…nothing.

There was only one other hallway Tommy knew of. He had never been inside it, but in one of his lessons Michael had told him that great things sometimes happened in that room. With nothing to lose, Tommy tried it. This way was open and he stepped inside.

When he first came back to heaven, Tommy had run a hand over his face and realized right away that he had been restored to his six-and-three-quarters-year-old appearance. He was once again much smaller than the adult version he had occupied for the last day or so. Now, however, he felt tinier than he ever had. For he stood in this vast expanse of a room feeling so very, very insignificant. Not only because of the magnitude of the hall, but because it was filled with people! So many. Tommy thought that everyone who was in heaven was gathered in this one place, and he truly felt awed and diminished by the billions of eyes staring at him. It was then that the most amazing thing happened. The vast assemblage broke out into loud and sustained applause. More than clapping, there were cheers and whistles too. From out of nowhere a smiling Jesse appeared. He took Tommy by the hand and led his friend to the throne of the Great King.

It felt like the longest walk of Tommy's life until at last he was before the Almighty flanked by the archangelic trio. Michael, Raphael and Gabriel rose and approached the little angel.

"Michael!" Tommy cried out. "I am so, so sorry. I failed you. I deserve whatever…"

Gabriel cut him off. "Did you contract some sort of human fever when you were down there? Whatever are you babbling about?"

Tommy wiped at an eye. "I failed. I revealed my identity to my parents, which you said was the most serious infraction of all."

Michael raised his mighty sword. Tommy winced until the sword gently touched the little angel's shoulder, and Tommy instantly felt—relief!

"No, Tommy," Michael said. "You did not break any rules. You see, you did not reveal yourself to your parents. It was they who spotted you."

"You mean…you mean I'm not going to be punished?"

"Punished! You are going to be commended. You performed magnificently!"

"But…but I did not convince five people to show purity of heart."

"Of course you did. You actually outperformed the goal."

"How?"

"Each of the people you touched committed acts of kindness that went against their own self-interest because of you. It was an astonishing display, one that we are all very impressed with." Raphael and Gabriel were nodding in agreement.

Raphael spoke. "Deacon John, George the former alcoholic, Dana the prostitute, the Pierces, Edward and Elena, Marsha, Angelo, Mike Talbott, the violinist, Marsha's family, your parents, and let's not forget Deacon John's daughter, another new angel (from a distance she waved at Tommy)—all these were touched by you and served a greater good."

Now Tommy began to smile. His smile reached ear to ear when he felt something growing out his back, and from all over the kingdom of heaven bells pealed. Looking and feeling behind him, Tommy was excited to confirm he had indeed sprouted angel's wings.

"Congratulations, Tommy," Michael intoned, and again the applause was deafening.

Looking at Gabriel, the little angel noted, "I thought you said bells don't ring when an angel gets his wings?"

"Fooled ya'!" Gabriel said with a laugh.

"And the Lord…He is pleased?" Tommy asked.

Michael replied that the Almighty was very happy. The trio of archangels and Jesse led the little angel to the throne.

The Lord God looked down fondly. "My little angel, I am well pleased. You have shown that there is much good on Earth." The Lord chuckled before adding, "I have to admit, watching you drive that car down the icy roadway had Me in stitches. I have not laughed that hard in at least three centuries!"

Even Tommy joined in the laughter at the memory.

"Actually you made Me smile quite a few times," the Lord said. "Laughter is a good thing—in humans as in angels. You richly deserve your wings. Thank you, My little angel."

Then the party kicked into high gear. Many said it was the Christmas party for the ages due to the great good spirits of the Almighty.

Several times Tommy asked if he could try his new wings out. Each time, however, he got caught up in tending to conversations with one guest or another.

At one point Tommy told Jesse that as much as he enjoyed this Christmas celebration, he desperately wanted to put his wings through the paces. "I bet I'm the first kid on my block with angel wings!" he exclaimed.

Jesse laughed. "Tommy, you are the *only* kid on your block who has wings."

When the party was winding down, Michael approached. "Tommy, I have something important to show you. You were not ready before, but now you are." When Tommy asked if he could try his wings first, Michael said this was much more important than angel wings.

"It must be another mission," Tommy thought. "That's fine, but I hope I can fly a little first."

As if reading his thoughts, Michael said, "This is not about another mission. It is of critical importance, however. Something about heaven you need to know."

"What else is there to know? This place is the neatest!"

"I take it you have not seen Gabriel's room. That is not so neat." But of course Tommy meant "neat" in a different context.

Just then Michael saw Jesse, who looked as if he would burst from holding in the secret. Suppressing a smile, the archangel said, "And Jesse, you may accompany us."

"Yaay!"

Tommy looked at his friend. "You know what it is?"

"Uh-huh."

Before another massive door, one Tommy had never noticed before, Michael said, "There is a great secret which is about to be revealed to you." He flung the door open, proclaiming, "Behold!"

Tommy's jaw actually dropped. He stood face to face with two smaller children—and his mom and dad!

"Mom! Dad! Oh, no, what happened? You weren't supposed to die so soon! What happened?"

"Tommy," Michael said, putting a reassuring hand on the little angel's shoulder, "remember something: There is no time up here. Heaven is made up of all the souls that ever were—and that will ever be. It is part of what makes the place endlessly fascinating. On Earth your parents still live, but in this place beyond time their immortal souls are always with us."

For the second time that day Tommy flew into his parents' arms with tears of joy. When he looked up he indicated the two smaller children.

Michael said, "These are your brother and sister."

The little angel hugged them just as fiercely.

He looked back at Michael. "They will all live normal lives?"

The archangel smiled. "Long ones also. I know it takes some getting used to. The idea that time does not exist. Just like God always was and always will be with no beginning and no end. In time you will be able to wrap your head around it. For now however, enjoy, and Tommy?"

"Yes?"

"Accept it on faith," the archangel said with a wide smile.

"Yes, sir!" Tommy's smile was equally broad.

For a long while Tommy and his family had a lengthy... well, it would be inaccurate to call it a reunion; it was actually a pre-union. Following the get-together, Jesse told Tommy. "Hey, I thought you wanted to try out the wings."

"Can I?"

Michael nodded, as did Mom and Dad.

Tommy looked at Jesse. "Where should we go?"

"The sky's the limit," Jesse observed, "but most angels for their inaugural flight find one trip more beautiful than all. It is one I happen to agree is particularly breathtaking."

Tommy did not know what it could be, but he trusted his friend and told Jesse to lead on.

"Are you ready?" Jesse asked.

"Like I never have been."

"Then let's go!"

The two took off as a happy Mom, Dad, brother, sister and the Archangel Michael looked on, beaming. They were not the only ones.

Far off in the heavens, God admired His creation. Especially what He at first took to be shooting stars. Until upon closer examination He realized it was Jesse and His little angel, streaking toward the planet Saturn at seraph speed.

✦ Author's Note ✦

"Every secret of a writer's soul…is written large in his works." If my experience is any indication, Virginia Woolf's words certainly ring true. There were times in writing *An Angel's Noel:* when I had a goofy smile on my face; when I could not see the paper (yes, I write the old-fashioned way) because of tears in my eyes; and when I closed the final scene, sighed and said, "Ah! That's nice!" If you experienced any of those emotions while reading *An Angel's Noel,* then I did my duty as a writer.

I cannot say if an angel guided me during this process. Certainly nothing overt occurred, though I encountered representations of angels at every turn. I am mindful that angels, like the Almighty, move in mysterious ways. I do state that I am a firm believer, as a Christian, specifically Catholic, that angels are all around us. Indeed, people much wiser have so stated. Look at the major scriptures, such as the New Testament, the Talmud, the Qu'ran. All are populated with the heavenly host. Angels are everywhere. Having said that, I lay no claim to doctrinal purity. St. Thomas Aquinas held that angels are independent spirits, and are not simply the deceased in another form. Despite that, I have adopted the popular conception regarding the transfiguration of the departed into angelic essence. Who knows?

The genesis of this story arose from multiple ideas that came together at "seraph speed." I posted something on Facebook to the effect that I love Christmas, cannot get enough of it, and bemoaned the fact that in modern society the twelve days of Christmas has morphed into twelve seconds. Facebook, with much of the vitriol appearing on a regular basis, also spurred the idea: what does God make of His creation? Do the evil and suffering in the world depress Him? And then again, there are so many stories, in social media and elsewhere, of that suffering. People, some close to home, struggling with sadness because of financial woes, health issues, emotional challenges, and the loss of a loved one. Out of these thoughts, *An Angel's Noel* emerged. If anyone going through a rough patch was cheered even a little by my simple story, then I could not ask anything more.

One note about the title. Throughout the draft writing process, the working title was *My Little Angel*. However after finishing writing the first draft, a quick check indicated there were five books by the same name of *My Little Angel*, all recently published, though none even close to this story line. Oddly enough there is no legal impediment to co-opting a title, but it still seemed wrong. Appropriately, a mid-day visit to a church sparked the thought of *An Angel's Noel* as a title instead.

Writing by definition is a lonely exercise, made even lonelier when you are an unknown author wondering if anything you write is sticking "out there" or is it all evaporating into the ether? I was blessed throughout by a number of living angels. Some offered sincere encouragement. Some took on more time consuming roles as I sought various sounding board insights. Still others inspired by their innate decency. While any flaws are mine alone, I am appreciative to all "my little angels."

I hereby acknowledge my deep appreciation of and fondness for the following. Friends who have been supportive and inspiring throughout: Larry Abowitz, Bill Katz, John McCabe, Mark Vorsatz and Raymond Freda of AndersenTax , Carolyn Slaski and Kate Barton of EY, Marty Flashner, the Lisbeth family, the Cutler family, the Raymond family, the Wallack family, the Manglass family, the Kvandahl family, Cathy and Jim Laffoon,

Raymond Zemsky, Gloria and Don Nolan, Marty Moran, Mike Wile, Sandi Maitland, Trina Albiso, Maria Contrerez, Diane Doyle, Jo Thierwechter, Sue Ann Cloar, Marvin Crawford, Keisha Sherrell Whitfield, Linda Marshall-Smith, Diane Etheridge, Maria Engemann , Dixie Elderjohnson, Christanna Springs, Suzanne Lydia Anthony, Mary Brymer, Wes Girling, and Phil Tatarowicz.

I was deeply touched by the stories of: Sandy and Ben Hernandez, Kathy Burke-, Joe and Joey Powers, Cathy Girling- and Bill Allison, Kathy, Mikey and Henry Zemsky, Mariane, Mary and Glen Morin, and Diane, Jimmy and Billy Kayser. As the Reverend Bob Saccoman, who inspired our little angel's iconic quote would say, "Those who believe in Jesus never see each other for the last time."

A special acknowledgement to Mike Rubino, who will be starting his second tour of duty to the Middle East. May the angels guide you and all our servicemen and women home safely—and quickly. A portion of the proceeds of this book are going to the wonderful people at Neurovation Labs; they have dedicated their professional lives to finding a cure for PTSD.

I also must thank Colleen Hughes, the editor of *Angels on Earth* magazine. She took time from an insane schedule to perform a random act of charity to an author in distress. If you have not done so, please check out Colleen's magazine. It is excellent!

A few people who graciously provided a forum to an unknown writer were: Barbara Wheeler-Bride of the *Busted Halo* website; Ryan Scheel of the *Catholic Memes* website; and Fr. Peter Stravinska of *Catholic Educator* magazine.

Throughout the production process, I again benefitted from an amazing team. Karen DeGroot Carter, an excellent writer (read her exceptional novel *One Sister's Song)* was a superb editor. Amy and Rob Siders of *52 Novels* magically transformed the typed manuscript to digital and print formats. Grace Anthony again amazed me with her artistic legerdemain.

Finally the greatest blessing of all: my family. My religious foundation was set by my parents, Catherine and Peter and my brother Brian, all of whom passed on way too soon. And the greatest joy of my life is my wife Gracie, and our children Richard, Marisa, Christine and Caroline, to whom this book is dedicated. You give meaning to God's good grace.

✦About the Author✦

Kenneth T. Zemsky is the author of highly acclaimed historical novels: *Knight to King 4*, *The Nation's Hope*, and *To the Close of the Age*. In addition to writing, Ken is a tax attorney with AndersenTax and teaches constitutional law at Rutgers University. He also taught religion to eighth graders (and has the graying hair to prove it) for thirteen years in his parish church, located near his home in New York's historic Hudson Valley, where he lives with his wife and four children. You can follow Ken at KennethTZemsky.com or you can contact him at KTZemsky@gmail.com.

Bonus!! Discussion Questions

The author has prepared a list of discussion questions for AN ANGEL'S NOEL. These are absolutely free. If you would like a copy, simply send an email to KTZemsky@gmail.com.